DOUBLE ESPRESSO DECEPTION

CLAIRE'S CANDLES
BOOK TEN

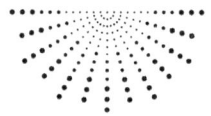

AGATHA FROST

PINK TREE PUBLISHING

Published by Pink Tree Publishing Limited in 2024

All characters and events in this publication, other than those clearly in the public domain, are fictitious and any resemblance to real persons, living or dead, is purely coincidental.

Copyright © Pink Tree Publishing Limited.

The moral right of the author has been asserted.

All rights reserved. This book or any portion thereof
may not be reproduced or used in any manner whatsoever
without the express written permission of the publisher
except for the use of brief quotations in a book review.

For questions and comments about this book, please contact
pinktreepublishing@gmail.com

www.pinktreepublishing.com
www.agathafrost.com

WANT TO BE KEPT UP TO DATE WITH AGATHA FROST RELEASES? *SIGN UP THE FREE NEWSLETTER!*

www.AgathaFrost.com

You can also follow **Agatha Frost** across social media. Search 'Agatha Frost' on:

Facebook
Twitter
Goodreads
Instagram

ALSO BY AGATHA FROST

Claire's Candles

11. Spiced Orange Suspicion

10. Double Espresso Deception

9. Frosted Plum Fears

8. Wildflower Worries

7. Candy Cane Conspiracies

6. Toffee Apple Torment

5. Fresh Linen Fraud

4. Rose Petal Revenge

3. Coconut Milk Casualty

2. Black Cherry Betrayal

1. Vanilla Bean Vengeance

Peridale Cafe

32. Lemon Drizzle Loathing

31. Sangria and Secrets

30. Mince Pies and Madness

29. Pumpkins and Peril

28. Eton Mess and Enemies

27. Banana Bread and Betrayal

26. Carrot Cake and Concern

25. Marshmallows and Memories

24. Popcorn and Panic

23. Raspberry Lemonade and Ruin

22. Scones and Scandal

21. Profiteroles and Poison

20. Cocktails and Cowardice

19. Brownies and Bloodshed

18. Cheesecake and Confusion

17. Vegetables and Vengeance

16. Red Velvet and Revenge

15. Wedding Cake and Woes

14. Champagne and Catastrophes

13. Ice Cream and Incidents

12. Blueberry Muffins and Misfortune

11. Cupcakes and Casualties

10. Gingerbread and Ghosts

9. Birthday Cake and Bodies

8. Fruit Cake and Fear

7. Macarons and Mayhem

6. Espresso and Evil

5. Shortbread and Sorrow

4. Chocolate Cake and Chaos

3. Doughnuts and Deception

2. Lemonade and Lies

1. Pancakes and Corpses

Other

The Agatha Frost Winter Anthology

Peridale Cafe Book 1-10

Peridale Cafe Book 11-20

Claire's Candles Book 1-3

CHAPTER ONE

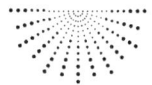

*C*laire Harris never used to let herself dream *too* big.

Why would she?

She spent seventeen years of her adult life working every hour she could in the candle factory on the hill. Single and plodding along, she would boomerang back to her parents' home whenever she couldn't make ends meet.

Well, there was one dream—a place she'd visit in the back of her mind during those gruelling shifts at the conveyor belts, sticking labels on jars like a faceless cog in a machine while BBC Radio 2 played in the background.

Her very own candle shop.

That dream dragged her out of bed every morning,

sending her to the espresso machine that would give her just enough energy to climb to that big old factory on that big old hill.

She hadn't been up that hill in some time.

Life changed for Claire Harris in her mid-thirties, and the dreams of the scents she'd create, the layout of the shelves with their colourful jars, and the window displays that would put her C in GCSE art to good use... they stopped being dreams.

The stars aligned when a shop became available in Northash's town square. That never happened, and even when it did, it wasn't like Claire's shop would magically materialise. She'd never had much drive, or so her mother had always told her, but the stars aligned, and she took that giant leap into the unknown. Another week, another day, even another hour, and she might have stayed at that conveyor belt.

She'd had her cake and eaten it.

Now? Surely, she was just being greedy.

To be in a relationship with her childhood best friend, Ryan Tyler? Impossible. And a mother figure to his two children, Amelia and Hugo? Unthinkable. And to be viewing a house... to *buy*?

Yeah, right.

Wake up, Claire.

Except, the stars *had* aligned before, and Claire Harris had learned to let herself dream bigger.

Just a little, as a treat.

"No bank will ever give *us* a mortgage, right?" Claire called to Ryan as she walked across the creaky floorboards in the back bedroom of Mrs Beaton's old house.

"Oh, they'd be crazy if they did," Ryan agreed, his voice echoing from the hallway. "It would be funny, though, wouldn't it?"

"Funny."

Claire stared at the expansive back garden. The overgrown greenery, almost jungle-like with its tall trees and dense shrubbery, created a natural playground for the kids. She watched Amelia and Hugo, now eleven and eight, racing through the garden, their laughter carrying on the spring breeze.

"That used to be us," Ryan said, standing beside her. He placed his hand around her waist, pulling her close. "It feels like yesterday, don't you think?"

"Sometimes," she said, twisting her sore neck. "Other times, I can feel the decades weighing on me. This holiday can't come soon enough, given how busy the shop has been this year." A soft sigh escaped her lips as Ryan kneaded the knots in her shoulders, his touch as healing as an angel's, his sports therapy qualifications evident. "The garden would look even bigger with the grass cut. My dad could spruce up the place in a weekend."

"I can see it now, like a painting coming to life," he said, drawing a little smiley face in the dusty window. "I could build us a patio for some furniture."

"We could host barbecues."

"And buy a firepit for roasting marshmallows."

"A treehouse for the kids in that tree."

"And maybe even a hot tub for us."

"Oh, how posh." She laughed. "I suppose there's room for it."

"It would work wonders for your muscles," he said, finishing up his massage by planting a kiss on her neck. "It would be quite perfect, don't you think?"

Claire turned from the window and took in the empty room. The cracked plaster walls covered in peeling floral wallpaper and warped floorboards weren't much to look at. And she wasn't much of a decorator, and even more useless at DIY.

"This could make a brilliant art studio for you," she pointed out. "Plenty of natural light through these enormous windows. Space for your easel and paints. It's double the size of your art cellar at your current place, and it's not even the biggest bedroom."

Ryan's eyes lit up at the suggestion, a boyish excitement that made Claire's heart flutter.

"I like the sound of that, but I'm not the only one with a hobby. We could split the room down the middle," he said, dividing the room with his hand. "My art stuff on one side, your candle-making on the other. A place to work on your new scents whenever inspiration strikes away from your shop."

Claire smiled, envisioning the shelves lined with fragrant waxes and colourful dyes, the worktable scattered with wicks and moulds next to her little black book filled with her secret formulas.

"You're right," she agreed with a sigh. "It would be quite perfect."

They soaked in the silence for a moment, lost in thoughts of a possible future. The distant laughter of the children drifted through the open window, drawing them down the creaky stairs, the wood groaning beneath their feet. Nothing some new carpet wouldn't fix, and once they had furniture in the old place, the echo of their footsteps would soften.

Not too long ago, it had been almost impossible to move around in Mrs Beaton's old house. Her former neighbour had let the house fall into disrepair, shrinking the interior by turning it into a hoarder's cave. There'd been festering mountains of bags bursting with anything and everything, sagging stacks of newspapers dating back years piled up as high as the ceiling, and dozens of feline occupants roamed around in their scrapheap haven among the chaos. Claire and her mother, Janet, had spent days clearing the mess before Mrs Beaton's eventual move to a nursing home.

Ryan broke the silence. "It's strange that she isn't here anymore"

Claire nodded, her eyes lingering on the spot in the sitting room where the tatty armchair had been by the three-bar fire. She missed Mrs Beaton each time she passed the old house on the edge of the cul-de-sac. The physical mess was gone, but memories of her old neighbour lingered, as did the musty scents clinging to the walls.

"It needs work," Claire said. "A *lot* of work."

"But nothing we can't handle. The proper tools, the right *YouTube* tutorials... we'd be a decorating dream team."

They continued down the hallway towards the kitchen where Sally Halliwell, one of Claire's oldest friends—and today, the estate agent—was flipping through an old scrapbook at the yellowed vinyl counter.

"I still can't believe Beaton used to be an opera singer," Sally said, tracing the tiny words. The newspaper clippings were so dated they looked tea-stained like Amelia's Egyptian history homework. "This 'Cressida Devey' sounded like an actual star. It's mad to think she had to fake her death at sea to get away from it all. And madder still to think she swapped the high seas for this house in this cul-de-sac in Northash, of all places..."

"Excuse me, estate agent?" Claire said, nudging Sally

with her hip. "Aren't you supposed to be selling this place to us?"

"Do I need to?" Sally slapped the scrapbook shut. "Without carpets, I could hear every word. Patios, firepits, tree houses, and a his and hers craft studio… sounds like you've already decided you want it." She hugged the book as she leaned in, lowering her voice. "And you know it's been on the market longer than it should have been. It's a *steal* at this price, but most buyers don't have the imagination. It could be as nice as any of the houses in this cul-de-sac with a little love."

Claire glanced at Ryan, gauging his reaction. They'd fallen in love with the big dream of returning to the quiet cul-de-sac they'd grown up in. Four bedrooms, two bathrooms, front and back garden… even with the work it needed, the house was the perfect place for them to start the next chapter of their lives with the kids.

"We want it," Ryan said, his voice tinged with hesitation. "*Really* want it… but the mortgage… we're not sure if we'll be approved."

Sally waved a dismissive hand. "I've seen people with less get more."

"Our deposit is tiny, Sal," Claire reminded her.

"Yes, it is a *little* on the lean side, but you have other things working in your favour. You've got a few years on the books to show the growth at the candle shop, coupled with Ryan's manager's job at the gym. And he's started selling his paintings at the gallery... that's three healthy income streams from where I'm standing." She rested a hand on Claire's shoulder and said, "So, what do you say? Are you going to take another leap?"

Claire glanced at the watch on Sally's wrist, the delicate hands ticking away the seconds.

"Is that the time already? We should get going." She gathered up Mrs Beaton's scrapbook, tucking it into her bag. "I need to check on the shop before we set off to the Cotswolds."

"I'm sorry I couldn't get the time off work to join you for the bowls tournament, but one lick of spring sunshine and everyone wants to move house," Sally said. "And don't think I haven't noticed you changing the subject, Claire Harris." She held up a hand, cutting off Claire's protest before it could begin. "Leave the details to me while you're away, okay? I know a miracle worker mortgage broker who owes me a favour."

"Sally, we—"

"I'll put together some deals, and then you can decide," she insisted. "I've got all your information, and I know I can make this work. You lovebirds deserve your dream home together, and I—Sally Halliwell, estate agent extraordinaire—will make it happen for you." She winked, holding up her little finger. "Pinky promise?"

Claire wrapped her little finger around Sally's as her chest fluttered at the idea they might make the dream happen. She glanced up at Ryan, and when he didn't protest, Claire nodded for Sally to work her miracles. With a quick hug and a promise to keep in touch over the week, they walked into the garden to join Amelia and Hugo.

"Are we going to get it?" Hugo asked, his eyes wide with excitement. "The house, I mean. Are we going to live here?"

"It's not that simple, little man." Ryan crouched down, bringing himself to the boy's level. "Buying a house is a big decision."

"But you want to, don't you?" Amelia, ever the perceptive one, studied her father's face. "I heard you both talking last night."

"Less of the eavesdropping, young lady," Claire said, suppressing the smile that wanted to break free. "But yes, we do. It would make a great home for all of us."

"And I think we can all agree that *I* deserve the biggest room," Amelia said with a definite nod.

"Do not," Hugo protested.

While the children bickered back and forth, Claire and Ryan walked around the side of the house to the front garden. As Sally drove away, they stood behind the front gate hanging off its hinges and looked around their old stomping ground. New neighbours lived at Ryan's old house, but Claire's mum and dad still lived at her old childhood home next door. Aside from the different curtains in the windows and flashier cars parked outside, the place hadn't changed much.

"It would make a terrific home," Ryan agreed, his fingers tightening around Claire's. "Back to where it all began."

"Let's put a pin in the dream for now. We don't want to be late for our holiday."

CHAPTER TWO

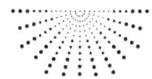

The sweet scents of her handmade creations greeted her upon entering her candle shop—aptly named Claire's Candles—as did the tension lingering in the air as thick as wax. Damon Gilbert, another candle factory long-timer she'd been able to rescue—and Sally's unlikely nerdy boyfriend—stood amidst a whirlwind of disorganised boxes and scattered candle jars. Bewildered frustration had replaced his usually composed demeanour—often found feet up reading a graphic novel or playing games on his laptop whenever the shop had no customers.

In the thick of it, Janet Harris, Claire's mother, whizzed about in her Janet's Angels cleaning uniform, rearranging shelves and scrutinising every inch of the space with her critical eye.

"Mother, dare I ask?"

"I'm just giving the place a bit of a tidy, love," Janet replied, her tone brisk, as though she had no time to stop and chat. "If your father and I are going to be running the shop while you're away for the week, I thought it best we start on a *clean* slate."

Claire cleared her throat and nodded at Damon.

"*Helping* to run the shop," Janet corrected herself, bowing to Damon as she swept past with a box clanging with candles. "Apologies, mighty leader."

Claire glanced at her father, Alan Harris, who offered a slight shrug from behind the counter as he flipped through a copy of *Lancashire in Bloom* magazine.

"I don't know how you cope with that storeroom being in the *state* that it is," Janet cried. "And don't even get me started on the filth behind this counter. When was the last time you cleaned under here?"

Before Claire could respond, Janet began pushing the counter away from its spot at the back of the shop, causing the tablet-computer till to wobble on its stand. Claire lunged forward, catching the machine before it could crash to the floor.

"Mother…"

"You know, the counter would work much better if it were closer to the door," she said, wagging a knowing finger. "You'd be able to greet every customer as soon as they came in, and then they'd be able to get out quicker once they've paid."

"I like to give my customers space to browse," Claire said, shaking her head—she wouldn't waste her breath defending her way of running the shop to her mother. In Janet's mind, Janet always knew best. "I want everything to be *exactly* like this when I get back, okay?"

"But if you just—"

"We've got a system that works for us, haven't we, Damon?"

Claire nudged Damon in the ribs when he didn't respond.

"Oh, yes," he said, pushing up his glasses. "Everything seemed rather clean to me, Mrs Harris."

"Which is why *I'm* the professional cleaner," Janet insisted, running her finger along a shelf beneath the counter. She held up her hand, displaying a minuscule amount of dust. "It's like Mrs Beaton's house in here."

Claire couldn't help but chuckle as her father shook his head, still flicking through his magazine while Janet worked around him. But there was no time to try—and likely fail—to stop her mother's neurotic ways.

A bright yellow car shuddered to a stop outside the shop in the clock tower's shadow. Eugene Cropper, sporting oversized sunglasses that made him look like a celebrity in hiding, leaned out from behind the wheel and waved. Claire's paternal grandmother, Greta Harris, waved from the passenger seat.

"All aboard the *Northash Express!*" he called with his usual theatrical flair. "This service will go all the way to the Cotswolds."

"Get the bags in the car," Claire said to Ryan with a kiss on the cheek before setting off to the stockroom. "I need to grab a few bits from upstairs."

Claire opened the door leading up to her small flat above the shop. She squeezed past the overflowing boxes filled with candles lining the staircase and into her flat, where more boxes had spilt out from below.

When she first moved into the shop, the storeroom—once the kitchen of a tearoom—seemed like more than enough space. Now that the shop had a healthy stream of regulars and even more repeat customers online, her stock levels had soared to keep up.

As a business owner, it was a pleasant problem to have, but as she squeezed past the tower of boxes half-blocking her bedroom door, perhaps her mother hadn't been too far off with the Mrs Beaton comparison.

On her bed, she found what she was looking for. Sid and Domino were curled up beside each other, napping away the morning. Domino let out her high-pitched greeting meow while Sid rolled onto his back for a fluffy belly rub.

"I'm going to miss you both too," Claire said, realising

it would be the longest she'd ever been away from them. "Be nice to Uncle Damon, okay?" She moved from Sid's belly to scratch Domino's face with the side of her finger in the way she liked. "You have permission to hiss at my mother as much as you like."

Domino meowed again as Claire pulled away, and a well-timed honk from outside stopped her from changing her mind about leaving them for an entire week. She turned to the door and noticed her little black fragrance book on her bedside table, positioned for late-night candle ideas. Next to it, a satchel filled with tiny vials of her cornerstone fragrances. She'd put the travel set together for if inspiration struck while she was away. But she hadn't packed it. Wasn't the point of a holiday to get away from work?

"Wouldn't hurt, would it?" she whispered to the cats as she scooped up the book and the satchel. She dumped both in her large bag—borrowed from the gym—and took one last look at the cats curled up on the bed. "You won't even notice I'm not here."

Claire bit back a yelp as she banged into the boxes on her way out, steadying them before she sent a tower of her fresh wildflower jars tumbling all over her flat. She took one last look around—the boxes had crept into the little dining area and the kitchen.

"Yes, I know," she muttered as she squeezed her way

to the door. "This would make a perfect second stockroom."

On her way down the stairs, she pulled out her phone and awkwardly typed a one-handed message to Sally.

CLAIRE

Try your best. I could use that miracle...

Back in the shop, Claire handed the bag to Ryan to load into the car and took in the glittery labels of her handmade creations. This wasn't only the longest she'd left the cats.

"Damon, Sid only eats the tins and—"

"And Domino has the pouches," he assured her.

Claire smiled, feeling more relaxed until she noticed her mother eyeing up the central Star Candle of the Month circular display.

"And keep an eye on Mother Dearest. You're in charge."

He gulped. "I'll try, but your mum scares me a bit."

"She's all bark," she assured him, though her tone lacked conviction. "Just... do your best." She went to her father, holding the door open, and said, "Keep an eye on them both, Dad."

"It's all under control, little one. You just focus on having a relaxing time. And take lots of pictures. I hear there are some beautiful gardens down in the Cotswolds."

"What's this place called again?" Janet called, scrubbing the floor in foamy circles with a tiny brush.

"Emmerdale," Amelia piped up, her eyes sparkling with excitement. "Where's the Cotswolds again?"

"No, it's called Perivale," Hugo corrected, shaking his head. "And it's down south somewhere."

"It's *Peridale*," Ryan corrected, nodding at the clock on the wall. "And I think it's time to set off if we don't want to find ourselves stuck in the lunchtime traffic on the M6."

After a final round of goodbyes, Claire held open the door for the first customer of the day before stepping outside. She took one last look at her shop—the lavender window display a vision for spring—before climbing into the backseat.

"Snazzy car, Eugene," she said as Ryan climbed in next to her, closing the door. "I've never seen you drive before."

"It's rented." Eugene adjusted the rear-view mirror and flashed her a smile. "And I haven't driven in a *little* while. But it wasn't *too* long ago... nineteen-something or other."

"You haven't driven since the nineteen-hundreds?" Amelia asked as she sandwiched herself between Claire and Hugo. "That was a hundred years ago."

"The nineteen-hundreds weren't *that* long ago," Greta said, and after taking a moment to think about it, added,

"You remember how to drive properly, don't you, Eugene?"

"Well, it's like riding a bike, isn't it? Only one way to find out…"

Eugene stalled within seconds of setting off, sending them to a juddering stop. The car behind slammed on its brakes and blasted the horn. Ryan and Claire exchanged unsure looks as Ryan quickly strapped the kids in with their seatbelts.

"Easy mistake," Greta said, her strained laugh not sounding so sure. "Peridale, here we come… hopefully."

"Bowls tournament, here we come!" Eugene announced as the car lurched forward again after the disgruntled car overtook them. "We're going to bring the trophy back to Northash… right after I figure out how to work this clutch."

Claire leaned against Ryan and whispered, "Did you look up the rules for bowls?"

He shook his head. "Did you?"

"I kept meaning too."

As they drove away from the familiar streets, Claire pulled out her phone and looked up 'bowls rules.' Even if they didn't bring the trophy home back to Northash, a relaxing week in the Cotswolds awaited them… if Eugene ever got them there.

CHAPTER THREE

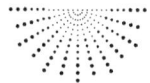

For the first time during the journey, Claire allowed a sigh of relief to pass her lips. Eugene brought the car to a smooth crawl outside a golden stone building fronted by a beautiful wildflower garden. A swinging wooden sign declared their arrival at 'Evelyn's Bed and Breakfast'. Claire's relief was short-lived, however, when Eugene yanked up the handbrake a fraction too early, sending them all straining forward against their seatbelts one last time.

The nearly five-hour journey from Northash in Lancashire to Peridale in the Cotswolds had been a test of endurance, to say the least. Despite setting off early, they found themselves stuck in the predicted bumper-to-bumper traffic on the M6. Eugene spent much of it grumbling about the sticky clutch and the awkward gears, weaving and diving between lanes at every opportunity.

"*Service station!*" Greta had cried, pointing at a slip road a few hours into their journey. "Lunchtime, I'd say."

Their bathroom and *McDonald's* break seemed to improve Eugene's driving somewhat. He even narrowly missed becoming the fifth car at the back of a four-car pile-up on the right lane, swerving into the middle lane with only inches to spare. Claire's heart had leapt into her throat at that moment, none of them daring to voice how close they had been to a crash that would have derailed their adventure.

"Wasn't that a stroke of luck!" Eugene had declared, and they'd all joined in the awkward laughter to fend off the panic.

But as soon as they entered the Cotswolds, with its tight, bending country lanes slicing through farms and fields, Eugene's driving became erratic once more. He vied for space on the roads with tractors and Land Rovers, his road rage uncharacteristically bubbling to the surface.

"If I move over any more, I'll end up in a ditch!" he cried at one particular SUV hogging the road. "And a good afternoon to you, too!"

To stop worrying about their imminent death, Claire had tried to focus on the picturesque scenery outside the window—the rolling green hills dotted with sheep, the centuries-old golden stone cottages with thatched roofs, the groups of retired people around every corner. She had thought Northash was quaint, but Peridale out-quainted Northash by a country mile.

"We've arrived safe and sound!" Eugene announced, peering up at the B&B as he turned off the engine with a twist of the key. "You know, I might buy myself a new set of wheels when we get home. I've rather missed the thrill of the open road."

"Thrill is *one* word for it," Greta mumbled. "I never doubted you for a second."

Beside Claire, Ryan's hand remained entwined with hers, as it had been for much of the journey. Hugo, oblivious to the chaos, had been lost in the virtual world of his handheld console, while Amelia had been colouring on her tablet with a digital pencil, her focus unwavering.

Keeping her opinions about Eugene's driving to herself, Claire peered through the front windscreen, drinking in the idyllic scene before them. The road stretched out ahead, past a bustling pub—The Plough—to a village green framed by honey-coloured buildings. A cluster of more retired-looking people in sensible clothing huddled together in the shadow of an ancient-looking church, their movements unhurried and graceful as they played a game of bowls.

"That must be our competition," Claire pointed out.

"One of," Greta said, squinting ahead. "Teams from all over the place are coming to compete, and they're standing between us and that trophy. I say we get checked in and start practising—"

A shrill voice cut Greta off, causing them all to twist in their seats. They watched as a tall, slender woman somewhere in her eighties marched past the B&B with fury in her steps, her navy pleated skirt swishing. She was chasing a man with similarly grey hair—though thinning—his eyes rolling as he strode ahead to escape her.

"Gordon, you *must* listen to *someone*," the woman implored, not one to be outrun despite her being at least twenty years the man's senior. "This plan of yours... it could be considered *cheating*."

The man, Gordon, responded with a dismissive wave of his hand.

"Lighten up, Dot. I'm simply *modernising* things for the new age. Like all things, we too must forge ahead and keep up with the latest technological advancements available to us."

"But we can win this tournament without your box of tricks," Dot cried, grabbing him by the arm. They ground to a halt where the B&B met The Plough, neither of them noticing their audience in the car. "If your 'technological advancements' get us thrown out of this tournament, I will hold *you* personally responsible."

Gordon's expression hardened, and he jerked his arm away.

"That sounds like a threat, Dot."

"Perhaps it is, Gordon."

He laughed, a sound as bitter as too-strong coffee.

"I'd be careful who you're threatening, if I were you," he said, scanning Dot from her sensible shoes to the emerald brooch holding her stiff collar together. "I'm not someone you want to make an enemy of. I won't hesitate to throw you off the team."

"You don't have that kind of power. My father was—"

"On the team in the 1950s," he interrupted. "I've heard it all before, Dot. Newsflash: as much as this village wants to stay stuck in the past, this isn't the 50s anymore."

"You rude *swine*!"

With that, he strode off towards the green, leaving Dot lingering outside The Plough, her shoulders rigid. She huffed and spun on her heels before marching after him, although she veered off into a building to the right that Claire couldn't make out from her distance.

"They must have been talking about the bowls tournament," Greta hissed, slapping the dashboard. "Did you hear what that dreadful woman said? *Cheating*! If one of the teams is employing tricks to make sure they win, I shall be having words."

"Hmm," Eugene grumbled. "'That dreadful woman' happens to be the sister-in-law I was telling you about.

Dorothy South. She's married to my older brother, Percy, and let's just say she's a firecracker. Fabulous, but a firecracker, and I don't envy this Gordon chap for being on her bad side." He chuckled as he unclipped his seatbelt. "Now, shall we get ourselves checked in? I need a little lie-down after all that driving."

"I think we all do," Greta agreed.

Greta and Eugene hurried up the garden path while the rest of them climbed out of the car and stretched their legs.

As Ryan hoisted their bags onto the pavement, Claire found her gaze drifting back to the village green. The bowlers were still gathered there, though something seemed off. Their movements had lost that earlier grace, replaced by jerky gestures and rigid body language.

Even from her distance, the rise and fall of agitated voices carried on the afternoon breeze. One man jabbed an accusatory finger into Gordon's chest, while another woman crossed her arms over her floral blouse and turned away.

"Doesn't look like this Gordon is winning any popularity contests," Ryan remarked as he hoisted his bag over his shoulder. "Do you really think he's planning on winning the tournament by cheating?"

"I hope not," she said, taking one last look before turning away. "I'd rather lose because we're rubbish—which we will be—than win because we've cheated."

"Speak for yourself," he said, giving a playful flex of his biceps. "I'm a finely tuned athlete."

"I don't think this is a sport you can win with your brawn. Hence why it's big with the retired crowd."

Claire turned to the B&B as the front door creaked open. A woman drifted out in a flowing yellow kaftan with a matching turban concealing her hair. An assortment of beaded necklaces clacked together around her neck, and her wrists jangled with chunky bracelets. Her smile was as serene as sunshine, and she smelled like patchouli and bergamot.

"Hello and welcome!" she said in a singsong voice, pulling them both into a hug with an arm each. "You must be the rest of the Northash team. The tea leaves suggested you'd be a little late checking in, but I've so been looking forward to your arrival. My name is Evelyn, the owner of this fine establishment, and you two will be Amelia and Hugo, which means the children must be Claire and Ryan. How lovely!"

"Other way around," Claire said, "but close enough."

"Such a beautiful family, regardless," Evelyn said, her cheeks blushing at the mix-up. "Please, follow me with your bags and I'll show you to your rooms. I predict you're going to have a splendid time here in Peridale."

With a tinkle of her jewellery, the eccentric B&B owner drifted back up the path and disappeared inside. Taking a deep breath of the flower-scented air, Claire followed, hoping Evelyn's prediction about their 'splendid time' would be more accurate than her guesses at their names.

Given the raised voices still coming from the green, Claire was predicting something altogether different.

Their family suite on the second floor, with a window overlooking the street, was as eccentric and charming as the owner. An eclectic mix of rich textiles and worldly trinkets decorated the room, creating a space that felt as warm as the spice of incense lingering in the air. A double bed sat against one wall, with two single beds tucked into the opposite corner—perfect for the kids.

As they settled in, a gentle knock at the door announced Evelyn's return with a stack of colourful towels.

"I hope you've found everything to your liking," Evelyn said, placing the towels on the dresser.

"It's wonderful," Claire said, inhaling deeply. "That incense burning downstairs… sandalwood?"

Evelyn's face lit up. "You have an astute nose!"

"I own a little candle shop back home. I haven't perfected my sandalwood blend yet, but it's getting there."

"A candle shop? How delightful." Evelyn clasped her hands together. "There's something so magical about the flicker of a flame as the fragrance dances through the air, don't you think?"

Claire nodded, reaching into her bag.

"I actually brought a few samples with me, just in case. This is my wildflower scent from last spring, made using local organic beeswax."

Evelyn cradled the jar in her hands, breathing in the delicate aroma.

"Oh, this is divine. Simply divine. What a thoughtful gift."

At the window, Ryan tugged back the curtains, flooding the room with warm sunlight.

"Is there anywhere nearby to grab a bite to eat? The pub next door looks a bit crowded."

"There's a charming little restaurant called The Comfy Corner near the library," Evelyn said, gesturing off yonder. "Or, if you're in the mood for something sweet, the café across from the green has cakes to die for."

Just then, Greta and Eugene appeared in the doorway, their faces alight with curiosity.

"Did someone mention a café?" Eugene asked, adjusting his velvet jacket. "That must be Julia's little place. Dot's granddaughter runs the place."

"Then off to the café we go," Greta said. "Cake sounds

perfect right about now. And let's hope that Dot woman is there to spill the beans about her *cheating* bowls team."

As they set off into the village, Claire found herself once again captivated by the magic of Peridale. The charming cottages and shops dotted the landscape, their facades a kaleidoscope of golden hues accented by a sea of pastel flowers. The old church stood proud, the oldest building around judging by the weathered stone.

Nearing the green, Claire noticed Gordon, the sole figure practising. He seemed deep in concentration, assessing the positions of the bowls while tapping his finger thoughtfully against his chin.

"Looks like he's using some kind of laser device to line things up," Ryan pointed out.

Claire acknowledged the oddity but found herself more intrigued by the village's allure than the unfolding bowls drama. On the nearest corner, a small post office with a queue of people long enough that it poked out the front door. And like a beacon, Julia's Café came into view, and the place was fit to bursting.

"I think that family on the middle table are leaving," Greta said, pushing open the front door with a rattle of the bell before waving them all in. "Get yourselves comfy before someone else snatches it up."

Claire's senses came alive as she stepped into the café, the enticing aromas of coffee, cinnamon, and sugar wrapping around her like a warm hug. Her mouth watered at the delectable scents, and she couldn't help but smile at the sunny yellow walls filled with framed pictures seeming to show the café over the years. While Ryan settled the kids at the table, Claire gathered the leftovers from the previous customers and carried the tray to the counter.

"You must be Julia," Claire said, greeting a young woman behind the counter.

"Jessie, actually," she said, and over her shoulder, she shouted, "Mum? Someone here to see you."

Before Claire could explain that she wasn't looking for anyone in particular, Jessie took the tray from her and disappeared through a beaded curtain into the kitchen. Left alone at the counter, Claire admired the array of cakes on display in the revolving cabinet. Each one looked more delicious than the last, all twinkling under the spotlights, their pristine decorations clearly the work of a skilled baker.

A moment later, a curvy woman with classic English rose beauty emerged through the beads in a pink apron. Her chocolatey brown curls framed a warm, friendly face with soft pink cheeks.

"Hello," she said with a smile that made her eyes sparkle. "You wanted to see me?"

Claire felt a twinge of embarrassment at calling her away from her work for the sake of a mix-up.

"Oh, no, it's just... we're staying at the B&B," Claire

said, hooking her thumb over her shoulder as the bell jingled from more customers. "Evelyn recommended we come and try your cakes, that's all."

"In that case, I should give Evelyn commission for all the customers she sends my…" Her gaze drifted to the side, landing on Eugene, and her face lit up with recognition. "*Eugene?*"

Julia hurried around the display cabinet and Eugene swept her into a hug, lifting her off the ground.

"Julia, my dear, you're as radiant as I remember," Eugene said when he put her feet back on the floor. "Marley sends his love, but my dear husband couldn't tear himself away from *his* café in Northash."

"Oh, that's a shame," Julia said. "I still have the vegan brownie he helped me design on the menu. Still a favourite around here."

"He'll love that. I'll let him know."

Before Claire could engage in further conversation, Dot, the woman from earlier, burst out of the kitchen and began making herself a pot of tea behind the counter. Greta seized the opportunity and approached her.

"Excuse me," Greta said, her tone firm. "I'd like a word about your bowls team and your cheating ways."

Dot bristled at the accusation, her demeanour less forthcoming than before.

"And what's it to do with you?" Dot asked, her eyes narrowing, but when Eugene stepped forward, her expression shifted to one of surprise. "You came! I didn't think you'd travel all this way for a bowls tournament."

"Excuse me…" Greta stood her ground, despite being half as tall as Dot. "We've come to take the trophy back to Northash, and we'll do so fairly and squarely. If your team is planning on cheating its way to the top, I shan't let such a thing happen on my watch."

"Yes, excuse you." Dot kept her attention on Eugene. "Percy is at our cottage, and he will be delighted to see you."

Without another word, she abandoned her tea and ushered Eugene out of the café.

"How rude," Greta muttered, watching them cross the green. "I don't think I like that woman much."

"She's harmless," Julia said, a hint of apology in her voice. "Mostly. So, what can I get for you? Since it's your first time here, the first slice is on me."

Claire settled on a slice of Victoria sponge and a black coffee, ordering a slice of chocolate cake each for the kids with a glass of raspberry lemonade to wash it down. A brownie and caramel latte for Ryan, and Greta ordered a scone and a cup of tea. As they sat down at the table, her attention was drawn to the conversation of a man and woman at the next table.

"Did you hear that, Robert?" the woman said in a low voice. "I *told* you word about the cheating would get out."

"Not to worry, Betty," Robert said, patting her hand.

"We won't let this go any further. We both know it's time Gordon was off the team."

Pulling her chair in, Claire shook her head at her gran, warning her not to jump in. They were both similar ages to Gordon, not long past retirement age. Betty had a short grey bob and wore a floral blouse, and Robert looked like a handsomer version of Gordon with twice as much hair. Claire wondered if these were the pair she'd seen arguing with Gordon earlier on the green.

If they were, Robert had jabbed a finger against Gordon's chest while Betty had folded her arms and turned her back to him. Before Claire could eavesdrop any more, Julia hurried over like a ray of sunshine, balancing a tray against her hip.

"I gather you're here for the tournament?" she asked as she dished out the plates.

"We are," Claire said. "Though I'm as novice a bowls player as they come."

"You and me alike. I had to dodge all of my gran's invitations to join her team," Julia said in a low voice as she added their cups and glasses. "I'm hosting a get-together here tonight for the Peridale team to celebrate tomorrow's tournament start. It's a little tradition, and since you and your team have come such a long way, you're more than welcome to join us."

Betty and Robert eyed them up from the next table, their stony gazes much less welcoming.

"We'd love to," Greta accepted with a hint of defiance—she'd noticed the stares too. "How kind."

Claire took a bite of the Victoria sponge, the fluffy texture melting against her tongue. She turned to compliment Julia on her baking, but the café owner had whisked herself back to the counter to continue serving alongside her daughter, Jessie.

Claire sipped her coffee, and she couldn't help but notice a peculiar scene unfolding on the green. Once again, it involved Gordon. A postman in a red jacket with grey shorts and a stuffed bag slung across his slight frame had engaged Gordon in what appeared to be another heated discussion.

"That man doesn't seem to have many friends around here," Claire said, placing her cup carefully on the saucer. "Are you sure gate-crashing their party the night before the tournament is a good idea, Gran? We don't want to ruffle any feathers."

"We were *invited*," Greta pointed out. "And it gives us the perfect opportunity to find out what they're up to. And they clearly *are* up to something."

Gordon, seemingly unfazed by the postman's agitated gestures, continued to assess the bowls scattered in a circle around the green. He moved with calculated precision, jotting down notes before making adjustments, as if the confrontation were a mere inconvenience.

As the postman stormed off, leaving Gordon to his

devices, Claire couldn't shake the feeling that they'd be stepping into a hornet's nest if they turned up for the traditional drinks.

Charming though Peridale was, a deep undercurrent of tension swirled around the home team.

CHAPTER FOUR

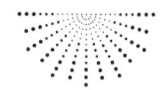

*A*fter changing out of the clothes they had worn for the journey, Evelyn offered to watch Amelia and Hugo for the night at the B&B, promising an evening of tarot card readings and tea leaf divination. To Claire's surprise, the children seemed thrilled at the prospect of exploring the mystical arts.

"I want to learn how to put curses on people at school," Amelia said, a mischievous grin spreading across her face. "Especially Mr Radcliffe and his smelly breath."

Hugo, not to be outdone, chimed in, "And I want to see into the future. Flying cars and AI robots taking over the world…"

"Well, my dears, we'll see what the cards and leaves have in store for you." Evelyn chuckled as she wafted burning sage around the room. "But remember, with great power comes great responsibility."

"You two behave yourselves," Ryan said, giving them a mock-stern look. "And don't go cursing anyone, Amelia. If I get a call from your school telling me Mr Radcliffe has spontaneously combusted, you'll be grounded."

"Fine. I promise, I promise. No curses... tonight."

Claire and Ryan left the children in Evelyn's capable hands and stepped out onto the porch where Greta and Eugene were waiting for them. They were dressed for the occasion: Greta in a floral sundress and Eugene in a dapper linen suit the colour of mustard. Claire and Ryan looked more casual in their own variations of t-shirts and jeans.

"Ready to uncover some cheating secrets?" Greta asked, rubbing her hands together.

"I haven't been this excited since my last amateur dramatics performance of *Fiddler on the Roof*," Eugene said. "Let's show these Peridale folks what we're made of. I hope there'll be champagne…"

As the sun set on the village, painting the sky in a palette of oranges and pinks, they set off towards the village green, where most of the Peridale bowls team had gathered. Gordon, the man on everyone's lips, strained a smile at their presence.

"Ah, our northern team," he said. "How… novel. Let me introduce you to everyone."

He started with Betty Fletcher, the woman with the grey bob and a stern expression. She struggled out a brief smile and excused herself to use the bathroom in the café. He moved on to Malcolm Johnson, a man as tall as a giant with a mop of grey hair who only managed a head nod. Next, he introduced Henry Morgan, the postman Claire had spotted arguing with Gordon earlier in the day. He held up a hand, looking the friendliest so far. Finally, he gestured towards the café, where Dot South and Robert Richards were seated.

"Lovely to meet you all," Greta said, fixing Gordon with a pointed stare. "We've heard some rumours about your team's tactics. Is this where you're keeping your 'technically modified' balls?"

Greta reached out for a chest and opened the lid a fraction. A red light radiated from within as a piercing alarm filled the green, echoing back off the buildings twice as loud.

"If you don't mind, that's private, for now," Gordon said, snapping the lid shut with a tight smile. "And we're not here to talk shop tonight. This is a celebration before tomorrow's tournament, when a dozen teams from all over the Cotswolds—and yourselves from up north," he paused, flaring his nostrils as though the thought of 'northerners' disgusted him, "will compete in the biggest bowls event of the year."

"I, for one, am excited," Eugene announced. "It's going to be a thrilling competition."

Claire, however, couldn't shake the feeling of apprehension that had settled in the pit of her stomach. There was something about Gordon that she didn't trust. She thought back to his interaction with Dot outside the pub and how dismissive he had been of her when he thought no one was watching. Now, with an audience, he carried himself with an air of authority that made every movement feel calculated. And the rest of his team seemed permanently on edge.

As conversation turned to the upcoming tournament, Claire stepped into the café. The familiar delicious scent carried her away for a moment, but the scene before her was far from the warm, inviting atmosphere she'd experienced earlier. Julia, the vibrant café owner, was hunched over a table, her shoulders shaking with quiet sobs as Dot rubbed her back in soothing circles.

"I'm sorry to interrupt," Claire said, wondering if she should turn around and leave. "Is… is everything alright?"

Julia looked up, her eyes red-rimmed and glistening with tears. She reached for a piece of paper on the table and handed it to Claire with trembling fingers. A missing poster, featuring a photograph of a majestic grey Maine Coon cat who answered to the name 'Mowgli.'

"Like from *The Jungle Book*," Claire said.

"He was so adventurous when I found him as a

kitten," Julia said, batting away a tear. "He couldn't spend enough time in the garden. But he always came back before night. He's getting old now, and I... I haven't seen him since yesterday afternoon."

"He'll come home," Dot assured her with surprising softness.

"But it's not like Mowgli to not show up for one night, and if he ever has, he *always* comes back the next morning."

Claire studied the poster, her heart aching for Julia's distress. She couldn't imagine the worry and fear that must be coursing through her at the thought of her beloved pet being lost.

"I'll keep an eye out for him," Claire said. "I'm sure he'll turn up. Cats are curious creatures, after all."

Julia nodded, wiping her tears with the back of her hand. She took a deep breath, seemingly drawing strength from Dot's comforting hands on her shoulders.

"You're right," she said, a faint smile tugging at the corners of her mouth. "I'm probably worrying about nothing. Maybe he's up at Peridale Farm, chasing mice and having a grand old time."

"That's the spirit." Dot gave Julia's shoulder a firm pat. "We'll canvas the village with posters all night if we must. We won't rest until Mowgli is back where he belongs, safe and sound."

Their bond reminded Claire of the one she shared

with her own grandmother, Greta. On the other hand, her mother's mother, Mean Moreen—a well-earned title—made Dot look like a Care Bear in comparison.

The bell above the door rang and Malcolm ducked his head through the café door with an agitated expression.

"Sorry to interrupt," he said, his gruff voice surprisingly timid for his stature. "Has anyone seen the champagne for the toast? Gordon's getting antsy out there."

Dot sprung into action, grabbing a tray laden with empty glasses and champagne already waiting on ice. One of the glasses already had a pale liquid poured in.

"The one on the left is Gordon's special elderflower cordial," she said.

"Thanks." Malcolm nodded, taking the tray from Dot. "Better to get this over with before Gordon has a fit."

As Malcolm disappeared back into the evening and handed the tray off to Henry, Julia tried to busy herself in the café, but she wasn't doing much other than adjusting chairs and sugar pots. If Claire had known her better, she'd have grabbed her in a hug.

"Let me know if you need any help with the canvassing," Claire offered.

"That's kind of you, Claire. Thank you."

Claire was reluctant to leave, but she sensed Julia wanted to be alone. She stepped out, the gentle evening breeze picking up her fine hair as she re-joined the gathering. Robert, the handsomer version of Gordon, popped the cork on the champagne, sending a stream of bubbles cascading into the waiting glasses.

"Quite the lively bunch, aren't they?" Ryan said as he handed Claire a glass. "Everything alright in there? That woman looked quite upset."

"Missing cat," Claire replied as Gordon's voice boomed with enthusiasm about the upcoming tournament.

She studied the faces of his teammates.

Betty stifled a yawn behind her hand, her eyes glazing over with disinterest as she looked everywhere but at Gordon. Malcolm kept glancing at his watch, as if he had somewhere more important to be. Henry, the postman, seemed lost in thought, his gaze fixed on the fiery hues of the setting sun. While the others at least feigned interest in Gordon's words with half-hearted nods, Robert was openly scrolling through his phone, his thumb swiping across the screen. There wasn't any urgency to his swipes; he just wanted to do anything but listen to Gordon.

As Gordon droned on about strategy and schedules, his voice filled with bravado and self-importance, Claire found her own attention drifting off to thoughts of the missing cat and where he might be. She sipped her champagne, wondering how far away Oakwood Nursing Home was.

When Gordon paused for breath, Greta drained her glass and cleared her throat.

"Since we *are* talking about shop," she started, "it's about time one of you explains what these *technological* techniques are that I keep hearing about."

The air turned frosty, the team members shifting under Greta's scrutinising gaze. But before anyone could respond, a strangled sound turned the frost to ice. Claire's eyes widened in horror as she saw Gordon, his face contorted in pain, clutching at his throat.

He staggered forward, coughing and spluttering, his body wracked by violent spasms. The glass of elderflower cordial, half-drunk, slipped from his grasp, spilling its contents onto the grass at his feet.

"*Gordon?*" Betty cried. "What in heavens are you doing?"

"He looks like he's choking," Robert said, slapping Gordon on the back. "Spit it out."

"Doesn't look like choking to me," Malcolm assessed.

Gordon dropped to his knees, his eyes bulging, and Claire snapped out of her stupor, her mind racing as she fumbled for her phone. With shaking hands, she dialled 999.

"We need an ambulance at the Peridale village green, immediately," she said, her voice trembling. "A man has collapsed. I don't think he's breathing."

As the operator assured her that help was on the way,

Claire turned back to the scene unfolding before her. Eugene, gulping down what looked like a mouthful of thumbtacks, knelt beside Gordon's limp form as the rest of them stood around shocked to stone. With shaky movements, he checked for a pulse, his fingers pressing against the man's neck.

When Eugene looked up, his eyes met hers across the green, and she expected the worst.

"He still has a pulse," Eugene exclaimed. "Hang in there Gordon. Help is on the way."

CHAPTER FIVE

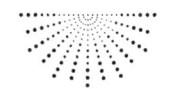

Claire shivered on the bench outside the café, her hands wrapped around a steaming mug of coffee. Ryan sat beside her, his arm draped over her shoulders, offering comforting warmth against the chilly spring night. They watched as paramedics loaded Gordon's limp form into the waiting ambulance, the flashing lights casting an eerie glow across the village green.

PC Jake Puglisi, a young officer with a serious frown that didn't match his boyish features, flipped back through his notepad, mulling over their statements.

"And you're *sure* you think Gordon Wicks was poisoned?" PC Puglisi's right eyebrow drifted upwards, his pen hovering over the page. "That's a serious accusation, Miss Harris. What makes you think that?"

"Because he was fine one moment, toasting with the team, and then suddenly, he was choking on all fours on the grass." She indicated to the rest of the team mingling on the green as they watched the ambulance depart in stunned silence. "It happened after he drank his elderflower cordial."

"Miss Harris, you and your team are from off yonder, right?"

"Northash."

"*North... ash.*" He scribbled the detail down, punctuating it with a stab of his pen. "And you're here for tomorrow's tournament. Rivals of the Peridale team, if I'm correct?"

"Spit it out," Claire said, matching his arched eyebrow. "My dad was a DI. I know a leading question when I hear one."

PC Puglisi shrugged, a half-smile tugging at one side of his mouth.

"Well, it's just a thought, but maybe one of you Northash folk decided to take out the competition? Gain yourselves a little advantage in the tournament?"

Ryan's arm tightened around Claire's shoulders.

"Come off it, mate," he said. "Don't be ridiculous."

Claire craned her neck to look through the café window, where she could see Detective Inspector Laura Moyes talking to Julia and her family. Claire would have preferred to talk to the DI rather than the PC.

"All I'm saying is," Puglisi continued, "it makes sense for you folk to want to kill off your competition. You're the outsiders here, and—"

"Gordon *isn't* dead," a paramedic called out, glaring at PC Puglisi as she rushed past. "Watch your mouth, Constable. Show some respect."

Puglisi's cheeks flushed, but before he could respond, Betty stepped forward from the green, her expression weary.

"Now's not the time for arguments, Emily," Betty called to the paramedic. "Though we know how much you like to make yourself heard." She fixed the paramedic with a scrutinising gaze. "Just get Gordon to the hospital, please."

The paramedic, Emily, muttered something under her breath that sounded suspiciously like, "As if *you* care." She joined her colleagues in the ambulance, slamming the doors shut behind her.

"What was that about?" Ryan wondered aloud.

"Not sure," Claire said. "Small village. If it's anything like Northash, everyone knows everyone's business."

As the ambulance sped off, its siren piercing the night, the café door opened. DI Laura Moyes emerged, a small vaping device clenched in her palm, glowing red at the tip as she inhaled. She watched the ambulance disappear into the distance, thick vines of vapour curling from her lips and disappearing into the night sky.

Claire studied the detective, noting the sharp intelligence in her eyes and the authoritative air she exuded. A far cry from the lumbering and always chuckling Detective Inspector Ramsbottom they'd left behind in Northash. DI Moyes approached PC Puglisi, her expression serious.

"What have you found out, Constable?"

"Miss Harris suspects poisoning, ma'am."

The DI's eyebrows lifted, but her gaze held less suspicion than the PC's.

"Why do you think this, Miss Harris?"

"It's the timing, Detective," Claire started, hoping to be taken more seriously this time. "We were all drinking champagne, except for Gordon. He had elderflower cordial. He collapsed after drinking at least half of it, while the rest of us are fine."

Julia appeared in the doorway of the café, hugging herself against the chill.

"I poured the elderflower," she revealed. "Someone brought in the bottle earlier."

"Then we'll have the glass and the bottle tested," Moyes said. "Who brought it?"

"It was there when I arrived earlier," she offered with a slight shrug, "but Betty Fletcher was rather insistent that I made sure Gordon got the elderflower and not the champagne. Said the last thing we needed was Gordon drinking alcohol before the tournament."

Claire followed DI Moyes' gaze across the green, where Betty was engaged in a heated, whispered argument with Robert. Malcolm and Henry hung back, tense and silent.

"Do you still have the bottle?" Moyes asked.

"It's in the kitchen," Julia said. "I'll fetch it."

But seconds later, Julia returned empty-handed and red-cheeked.

"It's gone," she revealed. "The back door was open, and it was on the kitchen island and… it's gone."

"*Gone?*" Moyes huffed, planting her hands on her hips as she scanned the green. "Right, Puglisi, I want every member of the Peridale team questioned at the station tonight. Miss Harris, no further questions, for now."

Claire slumped back against the bench, her mind reeling from the evening's events. The police left her alone, but their suspicions lingering in the air like a bitter aftertaste. She glanced towards the café, intending to ask Julia more questions, but the lights were already off.

"Let's find my gran and Eugene," she said to Ryan as she pushed herself off the bench. She left her half-finished coffee cup on the café doorstep. "I think we could all use a drink after that."

They found Greta and Eugene in Richie's, a quiet industrial-themed bar on the other side of the village green. The pair sat at the bar, nursing tumblers of whisky.

"To settle our nerves," Greta explained, raising her glass in a mock toast.

"Most macabre." Eugene shook his head, his usually jovial expression replaced by a haunted look. "I cannot *believe* something like this is happening *again*."

Claire's eyebrows shot up. "Again?"

"Last time I was in Peridale for my brother's wedding to Dot, our eldest brother was killed under peculiar circumstances in the village hall after the ceremony." He twisted in his chair and glanced in the direction of the church. "He was... frozen to death?"

"Frozen?" Ryan sucked the air through his teeth. "How?"

"You don't want to know." But Eugene leaned in and whispered, "Dunked in a vat of liquid nitrogen. Dry ice meant to look like clouds on the dance floor for their first dance. Our eldest brother wasn't the nicest of fellas—got himself mixed up with the wrong sort—but it was no way to go." He took a sharp sip of his drink. "Perhaps I'm the one who brings misfortune to this place."

"I don't think it's you, pal." The bartender, presumably Richie, a handsome young man, leaned in, his voice low. "Quite a few people around here say this village is cursed."

"Cursed?" Greta scoffed. "Who believes in curses?"

"Not me, personally, but let's just say the local undertakers do a roaring trade," Richie said, wiping at the bar. "Saying that, there hasn't been a murder around here all year... until today."

"Gordon isn't dead," Claire corrected.

"*Yet*." Eugene tossed back his whisky. "This is just my luck."

"On the house." He slid drinks across the bar to her and Ryan. "You're not from around here with those accents. Where've you come from?"

"Up north," Greta replied, taking a sip of her whisky.

"Want my advice?" His expression darkened. "Maybe you should head back there."

With that, he moved further down the bar to chat with Julia's daughter, Jessie, who was working on a laptop, leaving them to stew in his advice.

Claire slumped into the plush armchair in the B&B's sitting room, her mind racing.

"Maybe they'll cancel the tournament?" she suggested.

"If we leave now," Ryan said, sinking into the chair across from her, "we could be back in Northash by midnight."

"Absolutely *not*!" Greta cried. "We came here to win, and that's exactly what we're going to do. The man isn't dead, and we don't actually know what happened to him."

Eugene nodded in agreement. "And I can't leave

without spending more time with Percy. I haven't seen him since the wedding. That was already years ago, and none of us are getting any younger."

Claire bit her lip, torn between her desire to stay and her growing unease about the situation. Before she could voice her concerns, Evelyn hurried into the room, a tray of steaming mugs in her hands.

"I've brought you some relaxing tea," she announced, setting the tray down on the coffee table. "And if you'd like, I can offer tarot readings or crystal healing to help you process your ordeal."

Claire smiled politely, but shook her head.

"Thank you, Evelyn, but I think we'll pass for now. I was wondering, though... do you know of any connections between Betty and Gordon?"

"I don't like to gossip, but..." Evelyn hesitated, her eyes darting around the room, and said, "...Betty and Gordon were married for thirty years until recently. Everything fell apart around New Year's from what I heard."

Evelyn moved to the mantelpiece and lit the candle Claire had given her earlier, its soft glow casting dancing shadows on the walls.

"Thirty years is a long time for something to just end," Greta said, draining her tea in a couple of gulps. "Explains the tension. Why did they split up?"

"I'm not sure," Evelyn offered. "I have a feeling it was Gordon's doing."

"Typical man," Eugene said, toasting his cup. "Betty seems sweet enough."

"More than I can say for that Dot woman," Greta said, not letting her grudge go. "Where does she get off?"

"Kids, why don't you show your mum and dad what I taught you?" Evelyn said, calling Amelia and Hugo from where they had been sitting at the back of the room. "They've been proving they have the sight all evening."

Amelia shuffled the tarot cards with newfound confidence, her small hands manipulating the deck as though she had been doing it her whole life. With a flourish, Amelia drew a single card and held it up, her eyes widening.

"I *knew* it!" Amelia exclaimed. "Everyone on the bowls team will die!"

The room fell silent, and Evelyn chuckled uneasily.

"I didn't teach you *that*," Evelyn said, a flicker of unease crossing her face as she tucked the card back into the pack. "Ah, oh dear… maybe we'll leave the tarot cards for now." Turning to Hugo, Evelyn gestured to the remnants of Ryan's tea after he had finished. "And what do you see, dear?"

Hugo leaned forward, squinting at the tea leaves.

"I see a sun," he declared, a hint of pride in his voice. "It's going to be sunny tomorrow."

"How lovely." Evelyn exhaled, a smile tugging at her lips. "Ah, that's a much more joyous prediction."

"No, it's not a sun." Amelia peered into the teacup, her brow furrowing. "It's a solar flare, and it's going to destroy the village. Tomorrow. At noon. I can *feel* it."

Claire forced a laugh, trying to dispel the sudden pressure in the room. She glanced at Ryan, who seemed equally unsettled by the children's dark predictions.

"Alright, you psychic pair," Ryan said, clapping his hands together. "Time to brush your teeth and get ready for bed."

Claire knew the kids were playing around, but after witnessing Gordon's face turning purple before he dropped his glass, their words rang like an ominous warning. With a gentle smile, Evelyn excused herself, leaving the group to their thoughts.

Claire reached for her mug, mulling over Julia's words from earlier. Betty, Gordon's ex-wife, had been insistent that Gordon receive the elderflower cordial instead of the champagne. Could it be more than a coincidence?

"Strange tasting tea," Greta said. "What's on your mind, love?"

"Nothing," Claire replied, taking a sip. Its fruity warmth spread through her, but it did little to ease the nagging feeling in the pit of her stomach. "It's just... nothing."

Ryan yawned into his cup as he swirled his tea leaves and blinked sleepily. Eugene chuckled, shaking his head.

"That's Evelyn's *special* tea for you," Eugene

whispered. "Potent stuff. Best not to ask what's in it or where she got it from."

As Claire drained the last of her tea, a wave of drowsiness washed over her. She fought against the tiredness, her mind still whirring with the events of the day, and it wasn't long before they were all in bed. She struggled to keep her eyes open once her head hit the pillow, the room rocking like she was at sea on a ship.

Something was going on with the bowls team, and as she felt herself sinking deep into the bed—and she kept sinking—she couldn't shake the feeling that what happened to Gordon was only the beginning.

CHAPTER SIX

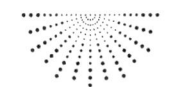

*C*laire awoke to the gentle rustling of fabric and the rhythmic creaking of floorboards. As her eyes fluttered open, she saw Ryan in the midst of his morning press-ups, his face a picture of concentration. She stretched out, feeling well-rested despite everything.

The aroma of fresh coffee and hot buttered toast wafted up from the kitchen below, mingling with the soft chatter of Amelia and Hugo. Claire smiled, picturing them helping Evelyn prepare breakfast.

As she sat up, the remnants of a peculiar dream lingered in her mind. She had been playing bowls in a misty graveyard, the clack of the bowls echoing eerily among the tombstones. Noticing her contemplative expression, Ryan paused mid-press-up.

"Strange dreams?" he asked. "I don't know what was

in that tea, but my dreams were very *Sgt. Pepper's Lonely Hearts Club Band* last night."

"Bowls in a graveyard," Claire replied, rubbing her eyes. "It felt so real."

"Maybe it's a sign that you're a natural at the game."

Claire tried to recall the rules of bowls from her car research, but her thoughts were hazy, the details slipping away like wisps of smoke. She shook her head, attempting to clear the cobwebs as Ryan sat on the edge of the bed.

"I think it's a sign that Evelyn's special tea should come with a warning label," she said, swinging her legs over the side of the bed.

"Well, I haven't slept that well in years," Ryan said. "I don't remember climbing into bed last night."

A sudden knock at the door startled them both. Greta and Eugene burst in, dressed in light linens and sporting wide grins. Eugene dropped into a clumsy lunge while Greta clapped her hands together like a drill sergeant.

"Rise and shine, sleepyheads!" Greta exclaimed, her eyes twinkling with mischief. "Get up and get dressed. The tournament is still on, and we have a trophy to win."

As Claire, Ryan, Greta, and Eugene arrived at the village green, teams from various corners of the

Cotswolds prepared for the tournament. Laughter mingled with the clinking of bowls and the rustling of equipment bags, creating a lively atmosphere that was both welcoming and competitive.

"Are we the only ones here under sixty?" Ryan said.

Before Claire could respond, Robert overheard the comment as he walked past.

"If only Gordon were here to see some youths," he said, his voice sharp with derision. "He's been trying to modernise the sport for youngsters for years. You're the future, apparently."

Without waiting for a reply, Robert strode off to join his teammates.

"Haven't been called a youngster in a while," Claire said. "I'll take it."

"The rule is you're a baby until you're forty," Eugene remarked, eyeing Robert's departure across the green. "Seems what happened to Gordon isn't going to be casting too much of a shadow. There's something about that fella that gives me a funny feeling. I wouldn't be surprised if he was the one who slipped something into Gordon's drink."

"We still don't know for certain if Gordon was poisoned," Greta reminded them. "Now, are we going to start practising, or are we going to stand around gossiping like a bunch of fishwives?"

"Oh, the second option, please," Eugene said with a giddy clap.

"Request denied," Greta responded, unzipping a bag containing their bowls. "Claire, grab the jack."

"Who's Jack?"

"*The* jack." Greta plucked the small yellow bowl from the collection. "And I *knew* it! That was a test, and you failed. You don't have the first clue how to play bowls, do you?"

"You throw them?"

"Okay, so you have the *first* idea," Greta said with a playful purse of her lips. "Didn't you practise at all? Starfall Park has two bowling greens to choose from. Much nicer than this green, if I do say so myself." She patted her pockets. "Anyone have a pen and paper?"

"Always," Eugene said, producing a golden pen along with a leather-embossed journal from his pocket.

Greta flipped through, scanning over the notes.

"'Hold the scream for three more seconds and stare off into the centre-right until applause'?"

"Amateur dramatics notes," he explained, turning the page for her.

"There's nothing amateur about your dramatics, dear." Greta flipped to a clean page and clicked the pen. "Okay, it's quite simple once you get the hang of it." She ushered Claire closer as she began to scribble a diagram of the green. "One opponent from each team will flip a coin to decide who lays the mat and rolls the jack. The jack is the target. You want to roll as close to the jack as possible, but this isn't skittles. You don't want to knock it away, just get close. Like Eugene driving us here, almost hitting every car that passed us."

"I did not crash."

"That's why I said 'almost'." Greta winked at him. "Each player has four bowls, and like I said, the aim is to get as close to the jack as possible. The bowls are weighted on one side, so they curve as they travel down the green, which is where the strategy comes in. You have to take the curve into consideration when you throw."

"Roll," Eugene corrected. "This isn't shot put."

"What about the scoring?" Ryan asked, following along.

"The team or player with the bowl closest to the jack at the end of an end—that's when all the bowls have been played—scores a point for each bowl that's closer than their opponent's nearest bowl," Greta explained, drawing a couple of circles near her drawn jack, and then circling the one closest. "The game is typically played until one side reaches a predetermined number of points or a certain number of ends have been completed. Usually twenty-one, but we're down south, so who knows how they do it?"

"So, it's all about precision and strategy?" Ryan said.

"Exactly, my dear. It's a game of finesse, not brute

force," Greta concluded, clicking the pen. "It's also supposed to be fun. It's a good-spirited game with the right people. Don't be surprised if you get a handshake for a particularly good throw. Claire…" She hesitated before patting her on the arm. "Just… try your best."

A whistle pierced the air, signalling the start of the tournament. The announcement of the first match, Riverswick versus Northash, fluttering Claire's nerves. With barely a moment to process the rules Greta had just explained, Claire found herself thrust into the heart of the competition.

"It's supposed to be fun," Claire repeated, looking down at her hands. "So, why are my hands shaking?"

"You'll smash it," Ryan reassured her.

"Break a leg," Eugene said, slapping her on the back. "Evelyn read my leaves over breakfast and said we're going to win this one."

"Oh, dear," Greta muttered under her breath as she polished her bowl. "Like I said, just try your best. What will be will be."

Gathering their equipment, the Northash team made their way to the designated area of the green. As they approached their opponents, Claire took in the determined expressions on the faces of the Riverswick players. The air crackled with anticipation, and the weight of the moment settled upon her shoulders.

"Riverswick rolls first," a man in an official-looking

polo shirt declared after flipping a coin. "Lay your mat and roll the jack."

One of the Riverswick players sent the yellow jack into the centre of the green. Claire started clapping when it ground to a halt, but she stopped when nobody else joined in.

"I'll go first," Greta said. "Watch and learn."

Greta, exuding an air of calm confidence, stepped up to deliver their first bowl. With a fluid motion, Greta released the bowl, sending it gliding across the smooth surface of the green. It travelled with a gentle curve, much slower than Claire had expected. As it came to rest mere inches from the jack, a cheer erupted from Eugene.

"We couldn't have had a better start!" he exclaimed.

The Riverswick team, undeterred by the strong start from their opponents, prepared to take their turn. Their lead player, a seasoned gentleman with a steely gaze, stepped forward. With a skilful motion, he delivered his bowl, the sphere cutting a graceful arc across the green.

As the bowl settled near the jack—though Greta's was still closer—the Riverswick team nodded in approval. The game was officially underway, and the battle for the trophy had begun.

The Peridale team watched on from the edge of the green near the café, and even without their leader, they were bickering among themselves. Someone needed to remind them it was supposed to be fun.

"*Claire?*" Greta thrust a bowl into her hands and pushed her onto the green. "Stop daydreaming. It's your turn."

When the tournament paused for lunch, Claire made her way to the café to order sandwiches for the team. Julia was behind the counter, dark circles under her eyes, slumped forward until she heard the jingle of the bell. She straightened up, plastering on a weary smile. Claire knew those mornings all too well, though hers were usually caused from one too many pints of Hesketh Homebrew with Damon.

"No luck finding Mowgli?" Claire asked.

Julia shook her head. "Not yet. I called the vets, and they haven't had any reports of his chip being scanned. They said that's a good sign."

In the sea of customers seated at the tables being tended to by Jessie, Robert and Betty engaged in a tense conversation at the table nearest the counter.

"You can't just take over the team without a discussion, Robert," Betty insisted, her tone sharp. "Gordon won't like it."

"To hell with what Gordon thinks!" Robert grabbed her hands, his eyes narrowing. "Come on, Betty. You don't want Gordon running the team any more than Dot,

Malcolm, or Henry do. He might have good ideas, but he's a tyrant. We *all* want him gone. Now is the time to make it happen."

"You're playing a dangerous game."

To Claire's surprise, Betty and Robert's fingers intertwined across the table, a gesture that seemed to convey a deeper connection between them. She averted her gaze, not wanting to intrude on their private moment.

Claire turned back to Julia, but she'd retreated into the kitchen, leaving Jessie to serve her. She picked out some sandwiches from the fridge and ordered a round of coffees to keep everyone's energy up. Back on the green, she made her way to the other side of the church wall, where gazebos had been set up for teams to rest during the games they weren't taking part in.

Ryan and the kids were settled on a picnic blanket just outside one tent, enjoying the shade provided by a nearby tree. Claire handed out the sandwiches, taking a seat beside Ryan as she unwrapped her chicken mayo on brown. Greta and Eugene huddled together, their voices low as they discussed strategies for the upcoming matches.

As Claire took a bite of her sandwich, her gaze once again settled on the Peridale team, something that was starting to feel impossible to resist doing. Betty and Robert had left the café, and they were all gathered in a tight circle, their heads bowed as they whispered among themselves.

Claire had the urge to go over to pick up on what they were saying, but she cut her eyes away when Dot locked on hers with a narrowed glare.

"Okay, we got lucky winning that first match," Greta said, pulling out Eugene's pad and pen again. "Claire, you need to work on your footwork, and your angles are all off…"

LATER IN THE AFTERNOON, CLAIRE STOOD ON THE EDGE OF the green, her heart pounding as she watched the Peridale team celebrate their latest victory. Their jubilant shouts and high-fives filled the air, a stark contrast to the anxious anticipation that gripped her. Peridale had already secured their coveted place in tomorrow's semi-final alongside the formidable teams from Bourton-on-the-Water and Oxford.

Now, the fate of the remaining spot hung in the balance, with Riverswick and Northash locked in a fierce battle. Each team had experienced the bittersweet taste of both defeat and a draw, leaving them on equal footing as they vied for the last position.

And somehow, the last throw came down to Claire, who, despite being a novice, wasn't the worst in the pack.

Luckily for her, Riverswick hadn't been in good form all day.

"Remember, Claire, it's all about the technique," Greta said, massaging her shoulders. "Keep your arm straight, your wrist firm, and follow through with your throw."

"Forget all that, Claire!" Eugene said. "Just roll and hope for the best. Riverswick's last bowl is miles out. You don't even have to get that close to win."

Ryan placed a reassuring hand on Claire's shoulder. Given his gym background, nobody was surprised that he had taken to the game like a duck to water.

"Remember your lunge," he told her. "You've got this."

Claire nodded, taking a deep breath as she stepped forward. Victory was hers to take, and she had a surprising sense of investment in a tournament she had cared little about before it started. She focused on the jack, her grip tightening on the bowl. She looked back at her team, and Eugene and Ryan gave her double thumbs up. She couldn't lay eyes on Greta. Perhaps she had gone to the bench where Amelia and Hugo were camped out, but there was no time to stop and search the crowd. The longer she waited, the heavier the bowl felt in her palm.

Clearing her throat, she dropped into the lunge, and with the smoothest motion she could muster, she released the bowl. As it sped across the green, she was sure she'd over-egged it. It curved at the last moment, striking the side of the jack with a satisfying click before grinding to a halt halfway between the jack and Riverswick's last bowl. Polite applause rippled through the spectators, but Eugene and Ryan didn't hold back their cheers. From the sidelines, Greta rushed in.

"Did I miss it?" she asked, looking around. "Damn my bladder, but I couldn't hold it."

"We *won*, Greta!" Eugene cried, picking Claire up off the ground. "Claire rolled a blinder!"

"That's my girl!" Greta exclaimed, her voice brimming with joy. "I never doubted you for a second."

Amelia and Hugo wandered over, looking less enthusiastic and unable to hide their boredom at being forced to watch the 'old people sport.'

"Well done, Claire," Hugo said. "You're better at this than you are my *Switch* games."

"There's still time for that solar flare I predicted to destroy us all," Amelia said. "But yeah, well done, Claire. What's for dinner? I'm starving."

The Riverswick team, though disappointed, offered handshakes and congratulations. Across the green, Julia emerged from the café, a steaming cup of tea in hand. She raised the mug in a silent toast.

But celebrating the victory wasn't to last.

Claire's eyes widened as a sudden, chilling scream pierced the pleasant atmosphere, freezing the festive air around her. A prickle ran down her spine, and her heart lurched in her chest. That horrified cry had come from one of the nearby tents.

An uneasy hush fell over the village green as the crowd moved towards the noise.

Something was wrong.

As they neared the tent, Claire's stomach dropped at the sight before them. Betty, Malcolm, and Henry stood around Robert's motionless body on the ground, his head bleeding, a dark pool forming beneath him.

Claire's heart sank as she recognised the lifeless stare in Robert's eyes. There was no mistaking it this time.

Robert was dead.

CHAPTER SEVEN

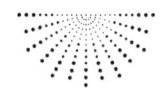

The once peaceful village green had transformed into a circus, with curious onlookers taking their turns to gather around the tent where Robert's body lay. The excited chatter from the tournament had given way to hushed whispers and speculation about the grim discovery.

Ryan, ever the protective father, had ushered the kids back to the safety of the B&B, shielding them from the morbid spectacle. Greta and Eugene huddled together, and Claire caught snippets of their conversation as they speculated about what could have happened to Robert.

"I *knew* there was something off about that man," Greta muttered, her eyes narrowed. "But I never thought it would come to this."

"Indeed, my dear. It seems our holiday has taken quite the sinister turn."

As Claire listened to their musings, she noticed Betty, who stood apart from the crowd, leaning against the church wall. The woman's face was ashen, her wide eyes vacant as she stared at the road. What struck Claire the most was the sight of Betty's hands, covered in what appeared to be blood. PC Puglisi, his expression grim, didn't seem to be getting much from Betty.

Claire's mind raced with questions. What had happened to Robert? Was it an accident, or something more disturbing? And why was Betty covered in blood? Had she stumbled upon the scene, or was she somehow involved?

DI Laura Moyes arrived on the scene, her presence commanding immediate attention. The detective strode from the direction of the pub, wiping her mouth with a napkin and brushing crumbs off her maroon blouse. With a few quick orders, she set about securing the scene, separating potential witnesses, and urging her officers to hasten erecting a cordon to keep the curious onlookers at bay. Late or not, there was no denying that she was a professional.

As Claire observed the proceedings, she found herself caught in DI Moyes' line of sight, and to her surprise, the detective cut straight for her.

"PC Puglisi mentioned your father is a DI," Moyes stated.

"Retired," Claire clarified. "But yes, he was."

"The best Northash ever had," Greta added.

"I'll second that," Eugene said.

DI Moyes nodded, and she seemed to respect this information. She looked off to the white tent as her officers worked on pushing the crowd back. Turning back to Claire, she took a quick blast of her red-tipped vape.

"What happened here?" she asked.

"The Peridale team has done nothing but bicker and argue," Eugene declared, his theatrical nature seeping into his words. "They've been bad sports all day. Have congratulated no other team when they've done well, but they celebrated like oafs whenever they won."

"In quite poor taste, considering their leader is in hospital right now," Greta said. "I know Dot is your sister-in-law, Eugene, but I know a rotten egg when I smell one."

"And Claire?" Moyes pushed, meeting her eyes. "What do you think?"

"They've been at each other's throats every time I've seen them. And they're not subtle about it. I heard Betty and Robert talking earlier in the café, and it sounded like they were happy to get Gordon out of the way for the sake of the team."

"Dot mentioned something about Gordon's cheating," Eugene added. "I wonder if that's how they won so many games today?"

"I wouldn't put it past them."

As if on cue, Dot walked past.

"It's because we're a solid team who practised every day for months," Dot fired back, her voice tinged with defensiveness. "Something your team clearly hasn't done. I know amateurs when I see them."

Without waiting for a response, she headed towards the café.

"The cheek of that woman," Greta grumbled. "Rotten, I tell you."

DI Moyes turned her attention to Greta and Eugene, asking when they had last seen Robert alive. Claire recalled spotting him merely half an hour ago, celebrating the team's victory alongside his fellow players. Greta, however, provided a more recent sighting.

"I saw him heading towards the tent just before Claire was about to take her winning turn," Greta stated, her brow furrowed in concentration. "Fifteen minutes ago?"

DI Moyes' eyes narrowed, her analytical mind processing the information.

"And what about the rest of the team? Did anyone see them around that time?"

Claire tried to recall, but she'd been too busy focusing on her winning throw.

"They'd all scattered by then," Eugene offered. "They didn't stick around to watch the last game play out."

"Bad sports," Greta muttered.

PC Puglisi approached them, his expression apologetic as he interrupted.

"I've just spoken with Betty, Detective," he reported, scratching the side of his head with a pen. "She's too shaken up to provide any coherent answers at the moment."

"She's got blood on her hands," Moyes pointed out. "I want her at the station for questioning, shaken up or not."

"She said she used to be a nurse," he explained. "It was her first instinct to search for the wound. To stem the bleeding. But she was too late. Body was still warm when she found him."

"Was she the first?"

"Malcolm and Henry said they entered the tent to find Betty crouched by Robert, covered in blood. That's when they say she started screaming." The young officer's eyes met Claire's, a flicker of remorse in his gaze. "And I apologise for suspecting you yesterday. Eyewitnesses have confirmed that you were on the green when Robert was likely attacked. It couldn't have been any of you."

"But where was Dot?" Greta pointed out.

All eyes turned towards the café, where Dot stood behind the window, watching the scene. Her expression was unreadable, a mixture of shock and something else

Claire couldn't quite decipher. The door opened and Julia approached the group, arms folded over her pink apron.

"Moyes, I've been wanting to talk to you," she said. "I should have found you earlier, but I've had a lot on my mind."

"What is it, Julia?"

Given their soft tones with each other, they seemed to be friends.

"I've been thinking about the sequence of events leading up to what happened to Gordon," she revealed, her voice tinged with worry. "I think he was poisoned."

"Can you confirm if it was poisoning?" Claire asked Moyes. "The toxicology report should have come back by now."

Moyes nodded. "Gordon had higher than safe digitoxin levels in his blood."

"Digi-what-now?" Eugene asked.

"It's a cardiac glycoside," Moyes stated.

"Again in English?" Greta asked.

"It causes heart failure," Claire said, without needing to think about it. "Is that right, Detective?"

"Yes," Moyes said, narrowing her eyes on Claire. "In high levels, it can lead to cardiac insufficiency, arrhythmias, and heart failures. Gordon is lucky he didn't have a heart attack."

"It can be found in certain plants," Claire continued,

digging in her memory for why she knew that. "The toxin, I mean."

Moyes' eyes narrowed further, but she didn't confirm or deny.

"We're still running tests to determine the specific substance used. But yes, for all intents and purposes, someone poisoned Gordon Wicks yesterday. The glass he drank from had surface traces of the toxin. Any luck finding the bottle, Julia?"

"It was most certainly taken from my café yesterday," Julia said. "Must have been between me pouring the drink and Gordon being taken away in the ambulance."

"Who brought it?" Moyes asked.

"I checked with my sister, Sue, and Jessie, and neither of them knows where the elderflower cordial came from. It was just there on the kitchen island yesterday afternoon."

"You said Betty brought it?" Claire remembered.

"I said Betty was insistent that Gordon drank it," Julia corrected, reaching into her pocket for a simple spiral-bound notepad. She flipped through the pages, her eyes scanning handwritten notes. "According to my gran, Gordon had a drinking problem as a younger man that almost cost him his career. He's been careful ever since to not go down that path again, so everyone in the group will have known about his preference for drinking elderflower."

"The toast is traditional," Claire remembered. "The perfect moment to pin down a time to slip a poison into a drink."

"Exactly," Julia said, a curious smile playing on her lips before she cleared her throat. Her finger traced her swirly handwriting, so neat it made Claire's own scribbles look as though they were done by someone with broken fingers. "From what I can gather, every member of the team had access to the elderflower at some point that night. I was the one who poured the drink and left it on the counter ahead of time. I wanted to be prepared because I was distracted by…" She sniffed back, flipping to the next page. "Betty and Robert were in the café at the time I poured the drink. They had access."

"And Malcolm took the tray out," Claire added, piecing together the timeline herself. "And he handed that tray to Henry."

"Your grandmother was also in the café that evening," Greta pointed out, her tone leaving no room for argument. "To leave that part out would be like baking a cake without beating some eggs."

"My Marley manages well without eggs in his café," Eugene added, suffering a sideways glare from Greta. "But I see your point. She's family to me, Julia, but fair is fair."

"Eugene, surely you don't think…?" she began, but her voice trailed off, uncertainty creeping into her words.

Claire offered Julia an apologetic smile, understanding her discomfort at the idea of her grandmother being a suspect. But Greta stood her ground, her eyes narrowed with determination.

"We should consider *all* angles," she insisted, her voice firm. "We can't rule anyone out at this stage."

"I think that's enough for now," DI Moyes said, already setting off towards the crime scene. "If any of you have anything else to share, don't hesitate to find me."

"I'll bring you a latte, Laura," Julia called after her.

DI Moyes gave a thumbs up over her head before she fought her way through the crowd while Julia headed towards the café.

"They're far too chummy," Greta remarked, her tone laced with suspicion. "The DI will never take Dot seriously as a suspect if Julia is on her Christmas card list."

"She might not be a suspect at all," Eugene countered, his voice calm and measured. "Dot is many things, but she's not a murderer."

"You're only saying that because Dot is your sister-in-law."

A short, rotund man with red spectacles and matching suspenders appeared with two dogs—one majestic and one dumpy—his expression one of disbelief.

"That's my wife you're talking about," he exclaimed. "And you're my brother, Eugene. I can't believe you're even allowing this suggestion that Dorothy killed someone."

"She's not ruled out," Greta maintained, though her tone was less assertive than before.

Percy turned to Eugene, with a glare of steel that didn't quite suit his cheeky face.

"Lunch at mine. Now."

They shared little in the way of a family resemblance outside of their eccentricities, but there was no denying they were siblings as Eugene followed Percy back to his cottage with his tail between his legs.

"To be fair, Gran," Claire said when they were alone, "where were you when I rolled my winning bowl?"

"I told you, I went to the bathroom. You'll know how difficult it can be to hold your bladder when you get to my age, love." Greta searched Claire's eyes. "You're not suggesting…"

"Fair *is* fair."

"You've got me there." Greta folded her arms, rocking back on her heels. "I went to the bathroom in the church behind the white tents, the same one we've all been using all day. I went in, I came out, I saw the celebration, I heard the scream."

"And you saw nothing?"

"Like Robert's bloody head after I bashed it in, you mean?" She arched a brow, letting Claire know how ridiculous she sounded. "No, I didn't. If I had, I would have said something. But, by all means, shop me to the police. I have nothing to hide."

"I believe you," Claire said, holding up her palms. "But in the same way that Julia believes her gran, it doesn't really matter what I think. If you suspect Dot because she wasn't around at the time of the murder, who's saying people won't think the same about you?"

"Hmm. I see your point." Looking around the village green, Greta shrank into herself. "Consider me a beaten egg, though, that's better than a rotten one. I still don't trust her."

"Doesn't make her a murderer, though."

"Doesn't make her innocent, either. Now, are we going to stand around like wet lemons, or are we going to do what Harris women do best and start sticking our noses in where it's not wanted until someone tells us something important?"

While the mystery surrounding Robert's death was undeniably intriguing, Claire couldn't ignore the nagging desire to return to the comfort and safety of the B&B to be with Ryan and the kids.

After all, she hadn't come to Peridale to dive headfirst into a murder case.

Claire pushed the vegan shepherd's pie around her plate, her appetite waning as her mind swirled with thoughts of the murder. The cosy dining room of the B&B, with its floral wallpaper and antique furniture, felt at odds with the dark cloud hanging over Peridale.

"I know it's been a crazy day," Ryan said, leaning in close, "but maybe we should try to keep ourselves busy? I reckon they'll delay the tournament until the investigation is over."

Claire nodded, her gaze fixed on her plate. She knew Ryan was right, but it was hard to shake the feeling that she was already in deeper than she'd like to admit.

"We could visit some of the nearby villages," he continued, his enthusiasm growing. "Do a bit of sightseeing? I heard there's a wool museum and some pleasant walks in the area. I wouldn't mind sketching a few places to paint when I get home."

Amelia, who had been picking at her own dinner, looked up with a frown. Hugo, lost in his handheld console, didn't bother to glance up at the suggestion.

"Boring," she muttered. "Are there no theme parks?"

"Surprisingly not."

Claire forced a smile, appreciating Ryan's efforts to distract her. She nodded, trying to muster some enthusiasm for the idea of exploring the Cotswolds. But even as she agreed, her mind kept drifting back to the tent. The image of Robert's lifeless body sprawled on the floor flashed through her mind. Claire sighed, pushing her plate away.

"What's on your mind?" he asked.

She hesitated for a moment. She hadn't wanted dinner to be about what happened earlier, but how could it not be?

"It's Betty," she said, her brow furrowed. "Evelyn said Betty and Gordon used to be a couple. And then, in the café, I saw her fingers intertwining with Robert's, just before his death."

"One woman, two men attacked. You think she might be at the centre of it all?"

"It's an idea."

Before she could elaborate further, Evelyn appeared at their table, ready to clear away their plates.

"Can I interest you in some dessert?" she asked, her voice warm and inviting. "It's a blueberry chia seed pudding. One of my favourites, as long as I have toothpicks on hand. Those sneaky chia seeds do like to burrow their way in."

But Claire, usually one to jump at the chance for something sweet, found her appetite had vanished. She looked up at Evelyn, a sudden thought occurring to her.

"Actually, Evelyn, I was wondering if you could tell me more about Betty and Gordon," she asked, her tone cautious. "Thirty years together, you said?"

Evelyn's smile faltered, and she seemed apprehensive about divulging any information.

"It's really not my place to discuss the misery of others," she began, glancing around as if to ensure no one else was listening. "The word around the village at the time was that Betty left Gordon for Robert."

Claire nodded. Given what she'd seen of their intertwining fingers in the café, it made sense. They'd been by each other's side at every given moment. No wonder Betty had looked so distraught when PC Puglisi had tried to extract answers from her.

"Gordon and Robert used to be best friends, you know," Evelyn continued with a sigh. "For about as long as Gordon was married to Betty. I think they came up in the same company together. One of them ended up being the other's boss, but I can't remember which way around it was."

"I'm sure the police will get to the bottom of what's going on," Ryan said, thanking Evelyn with a nod. "DI Moyes seems to be capable."

"Better than who she replaced," Evelyn whispered. "If DI Christie was still running things around here, he'd have had you both in cells for just being on a rival team before the day was over."

Evelyn left them alone, and Claire's mind was back to racing at the thought of Betty leaving her husband for his best friend. One poisoned, and another murdered.

"Time for a change of scenery," Claire conceded after a moment. "Why don't we head out for a little post-dinner walk? If the café is still open, we can grab some cakes for dessert from there."

"Great idea," Ryan said. "Get your shoes on, kids. And put your coats on while you're up there. It's forecast to be a chilly night."

Claire did want to make the most of their week in the Cotswolds, but even as she laced up her shoes on the bed, Betty, Gordon, and Robert lingered at the edges of her mind, refusing to release their grip on her imagination.

They walked through the village, the night air verging on the icy side of chilly. As they passed the red phone box outside the post office on the corner, Claire looked ahead at the crime scene, lit up by the police as they continued their investigation. Maybe they'd already found their answers and were wrapping up the loose ends so they could charge someone.

"Looks like we're not the only ones who had the same idea," Ryan said.

Greta and Eugene were on the other side of the post office, peering down an alley between the café and the post office. Curiosity piqued, Claire and Ryan snuck up behind them, their footsteps soft on the cobblestones. In a sudden move, they reached out and tapped Greta and Eugene on the shoulders, causing them to jump and spin around.

Before anyone could speak, the rumble of an engine silenced them. Julia drove out behind the wheel of a vintage aqua blue car, a relic from the 1960s that would have looked out of place with anyone else behind the wheel. From the little Claire knew of Julia so far, it suited her. Julia spotted them and held up a hand in greeting, and Claire returned the wave.

She watched her go, a twinge of disappointment in her chest. As much as she'd wanted to go on a stroll, she had been hoping to pick Julia's brain. Given that she'd already filled half a notepad with her ideas, the café owner seemed to be switched on.

"I don't think I trust her either," Greta said.

Claire turned to her, shocked by the sudden declaration.

"Why not?"

"We just overheard Julia talking with her daughter. They were saying they're going to look into the case to make sure they clear Dot's name."

"From what I could gather," Eugene took over, "when Julia tried to quiz her gran about where she was around the time of Robert's death, Dot was evasive."

"They're up to something. The lot of them."

Claire wasn't so sure about her gran's accusation

against Julia—or Dot, for that matter—but there'd be no convincing Greta otherwise when she had that determined look in her eyes. She had to do something before her gran waded in and made things look worse for herself, but what? There was only one person who'd know the exact right thing to say.

"I'll catch you up," Claire said, reaching for her phone. "I'm going to call home and see how things are doing there."

Claire leaned against the red phone box, the cool metal pressing into her back as she watched Greta, Eugene, Ryan, and the kids continue their walk. She dialled her home phone number at the cul-de-sac, unchanged from the days of her childhood. After a few rings, her mother's voice crackled through the speaker.

"Claire! How's the holiday going?"

"It's been... *interesting*," Claire replied, choosing her words carefully. "How's the shop doing?"

"Shipshape and as clean as a whistle," Janet declared, "but I was quite concerned by the state of your flat when I went up to feed Sid and Domino, but rest assured, it'll be spick and span when you get back."

"Mother, you really don't have to..." Claire said, pinching the bridge of her nose at the thought of her mother rummaging through her things. "Is Dad around? I was hoping to ask him something."

"Three guesses where he is."

There was a moment of silence before her mother's voice echoed around the hallway, calling for Alan. Claire perched on the edge of a flower box, the scent of petunias wafting around her. She imagined her father getting up from his potting desk in his shed at the bottom of the garden before shuffling up the garden path to the house. After a minute, his warm voice came through the speaker.

"Evening, little one. How's tricks?"

"Tricky. Potting anything good in the shed?"

"Just propagating some clippings of the houseplants before your mother kills them all off by over-watering them." He chuckled, and in a quieter voice, said, "But judging by the tone of your voice, you didn't call to talk about plants. What's on your mind? Homesick?"

"A little," she said, suddenly wishing she was with him in his shed at the bottom of the garden sat on her upturned plant pot in the corner. "Seen anything about the Cotswolds on the news today?"

"Not that I noticed."

Claire poured out the events of the past few days, from Gordon's poisoning to Robert's murder. She confided in her father about her suspicions, how things just weren't adding up.

"What would you do, Dad?"

"You know what I'd do, little one."

"Pay attention," Claire said, a smile tugging at her lips.

"Precisely," Alan confirmed. "Keep your eyes and ears open, love. You've got good instincts. Trust them. And if all else fails, you could always look the other way." He paused, before adding, "But I know you won't. And keep an eye on my mother. She doesn't want to make things harder for herself."

With renewed determination, Claire thanked her father and hung up. She hurried to catch up with the others, her mind whirring with possibilities. As she reached the edge of the village green, she noticed a film crew setting up, the crime scene visible in the background.

A reporter, her hair coiffed to the heavens and her suit crisp, stood in front of the camera, a microphone in hand. As the group drew closer, the reporter's words drifted through the evening air.

"…according to local police, the victim—a Mr Robert Richards—was struck over the head with a blunt object. Possibly one of the very bowling bowls used in today's tournament that was so cruelly disturbed by the shocking scenes here in Peridale this afternoon. Police are still searching for the murder weapon and are urging anyone with any information to come forward."

Claire had already shared what she knew with DI Moyes and PC Puglisi, but the reporter's words sparked a new line of thought. The murder weapon was a bowling bowl? It seemed more than plausible, given the setting of the crime.

As they walked in a loop around the green, they passed Dot's cottage. A pair of binoculars tweaked through the net curtains at one of the upstairs windows.

"There's a murder weapon out there somewhere," Claire said. "If the reporter is right, a bowling bowl. Want to bet the Peridale team has one missing from their set?"

"I'd bet my pension," Greta declared. "But the question is, what are we going to do about it?"

"Follow Dot's lead." Claire's lips pressed into a determined line, nodding up to the binoculars, tracking their movements. "We pay attention. And we start by talking to the other members of the team."

"Great idea," Eugene said. "Who first?"

"The woman found with blood on her hands."

CHAPTER EIGHT

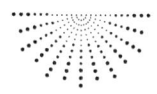

The early morning sun streamed through the café's windows, casting a warm glow over the cosy interior. Julia was nowhere to be seen, and the café was being run by Jessie and another woman whom Jessie kept referring to as 'Sue.'

To keep her mind active, Claire jotted notes in her little black book, not on the mystery, but on a candle formula inspired by the scents of the café. Ever since first catching a whiff of the place, Claire had been itching to capture its essence. She pulled out her travelling kit of fragrance oils, meditating over which combinations might best recreate the inviting atmosphere.

"Amy, did you hear?" a woman in a colourful sari said. "Gordon's been discharged."

"Dot called me first thing, Shilpa," Amy replied. "The man is lucky to be alive. Where does he live these days?"

"Since the divorce?" Shilpa replied. "I heard he'd moved to the nursing home. He's probably a bit young, but different strokes for different folks, I suppose."

"If you've got the money, they wait on you hand and foot at that place. I *wish* I could afford it."

Packing up her notepad after finishing her coffee, Claire approached the counter where Jessie was working on a laptop. The café had been packed when Claire first arrived earlier that morning, but it had soon quieted down as the tedious gossip spun around in circles.

"Jessie, isn't it?" Claire said, offering a smile as she handed over her cup. "Writing anything good?"

"Article for *The Peridale Post*," she said, barely looking up. "Split my time between here and there."

"Is it about Robert's death?"

"Yep." Jessie glanced up with a tight smile, and no more information was forthcoming. "Did you want some cake to take away?"

"Actually, there was something. Is there more than one nursing home around here?"

"Tons."

"And where would someone go if they wanted to be waited on hand and foot?"

"Oakwood Nursing Home," she said, her typing

speeding up. "Just on the outskirts of the village. Head towards Wellington Heights, and you'll see a sign for it."

"And Wellington Heights is…?"

Jessie glanced up, pointing right.

"That way." Claire nodded, not wanting to distract the girl from her work any further. "Thanks for the tip."

Claire stepped out of the café, a plan forming in her mind. She popped into the post office next door and picked up two bunches of flowers before taking a right turn and walking past the pub and the B&B. Rather than trying to use her nose, she opened a map on her phone. She followed the winding country road, cutting through a field roaming with sheep. After a pleasant fifteen-minute walk, she came to an 'Oakwood Residential Care' sign at the bottom of a long, tree-lined driveway. Another five minutes later, walking under the shade of the white blossoms above, a stately home came into view.

"Not a bad place to end up."

Pushing through the heavy front doors, the lobby was all dark wood panels and oil paintings in gilded frames. Behind the reception desk, two nurses in pale blue scrubs were locked in hushed conversation, oblivious to Claire's arrival. She waited for a moment, clutching the bouquets until they noticed her.

"I've always said it's not right," whispered the older nurse—her name badge read Celia. "Mr Wicks is *far* too old for her, and I think it every time she visits."

The younger nurse nudged Celia and nodded towards Claire, bringing their gossip session to an abrupt halt.

"Can we help you?"

"I'm here to see Gordon Wicks," Claire began, holding up the flowers. "I'm dropping these off for him."

"That way."

Claire hadn't expected to gain entry without question, but she wasn't going to linger around for them to probe. She followed the signs through the grand corridors, her footsteps echoing on the polished wooden floors. The scent of fresh flowers and antiseptic hung in the air as she made her way to the lounge area.

After a little scanning, she found Gordon sitting in a plush armchair, looking pale and drawn in the afternoon sun pouring in from a floor-to-ceiling window. Beyond him, fellow residents were battling it out on a tennis court with a cruel amount of energy, given what he'd been through. Betty hovered over him, adjusting his blanket and fluffing his pillows. Gordon waved her away with a weak gesture as Claire approached.

"These are from the Northash team," Claire said, holding out one of the bunches of flowers. "We wanted to express our sympathies for what happened to you, and we're wishing you a speedy recovery."

Gordon accepted the flowers with a wince, his movements stiff. He glanced at them before dumping them on a side table. Betty darted to stop them from rolling onto the floor.

"Thank you," he murmured, his voice hoarse. "No expense spared."

"It's a kind gesture," Betty said with an exhausted sigh. "I'll go and put them in water before they wilt."

As she hurried off, Claire seized the opportunity to probe further. She perched on a footstool next to him and watched the tennis players for a moment. There were tennis courts at Starfall Park, but like most sports, Claire was hopeless with a racket.

"Nice place," she said. "You're lucky."

"You think I'm lucky?" Gordon muttered, a cough taking over. "Someone tried to *kill* me."

"I know, I didn't mean… I…" She sighed. That's not what she'd meant, but she'd started on the wrong foot. "Thankfully, you lived to tell the tale."

"Unlike Robert, you mean?"

"I suppose, yes."

"Hmm." Gordon glanced at the tennis players. "I suppose you're right."

"I'm sorry for your loss. I heard you were colleagues. Friends, even?"

"I'm not answering any more questions," he stated with blunt force. "The police have been harassing me all morning, and I've had enough. I've been through an ordeal… I'm tired."

With a grunt of effort, he pushed himself to his feet, leaning on a wooden walking stick. He gave Claire a curt nod before shuffling off into the depths of the nursing home, leaving her alone in the lounge.

Betty whizzed back in with the flowers in a crystal vase, placing them on a nearby side table. She turned to Claire, her lips pressed into a tight smile.

"Thank you again for the flowers." Her tone hinted at a polite dismissal, but Claire wasn't ready to leave just yet.

"I wanted to see how you were doing, too," Claire said, her voice soft with concern. "After everything that's happened..."

"I'm shaken up," Betty admitted, gripping the arm of the chair. "Gordon thinks someone is targeting the whole team and that we should all watch our backs." She shook her head, a mirthless laugh escaping her lips. "It's *ludicrous*. There's no connection."

"But there is a connection, isn't there? The team. Their careers." She paused, wondering how far she should push it. "You."

Betty's head snapped towards Claire, her eyes narrowing.

"What are you implying?"

"I heard you were married to Gordon and had an affair with Robert."

"People do like to gossip, don't they?" Betty's cheeks flushed a hot scarlet. "I am *still* married to Gordon, but we've been separated all year." She paused, staring out at the tennis match. "Robert isn't the reason we separated."

"What was?"

"I don't see how that's any of your business."

Fair. None of this was, but Claire had made finding out the truth her business.

"Robert and Gordon used to work together."

"They did. Robert was Gordon's manager at a company that manufactured lasers," Betty confirmed, her fingernails puckering the chair's fabric as she clenched tighter. "Robert would always accuse Gordon of trying to micromanage him, despite the hierarchy. If they hadn't known everyone for as many years as they did, Robert would have fired him when he won the promotion."

"Seems like Gordon has been micromanaging your team."

Betty didn't deny the accusation, her silence speaking volumes. Claire sensed that there was much more to the story, but she knew pushing too hard could cause Betty to shut down like Gordon had. Still, Betty didn't leave. Perhaps she was weary of the burden of suspicion falling on her—the police must have wrung her out with their questions.

"It seems convenient to pin this on me," Betty said at last, turning to meet Claire's eyes. "But I'm not the only one who had issues with Robert and Gordon." She paused, worrying her bottom lip with her teeth. "You should talk to Malcolm Johnson. He's something of a recluse, and he's been coming to blows with Gordon a lot as of late."

Claire's interest was piqued by this new information. She recalled the stern, tall man who'd seemed timid while asking for champagne.

"Did he have problems with Robert?"

Betty sighed, brushing a strand of grey hair from her face.

"For all of his complaints about Gordon's leadership style, Robert was all for the new technology. He helped to develop it, after all." She shook her head in disapproval. "Robert was primed to take over if Gordon ever stepped down. I heard Malcolm thought he'd make a better leader."

As she pondered her next move, a hauntingly familiar melody drifted through the nursing home's corridors. The warbling voice, rich with vibrato, sang an aria that Claire recognised from her limited knowledge of opera.

"Gordon said that loopy woman warbles day and night," Betty muttered under her breath. "Anyway, it's time I was home, but please, talk to Malcolm. I live in an apartment at Wellington Heights on the other side of the village. Malcolm's cottage is on the way. Like I said, he's something of a recluse so he might not open the door to you, but I can show you where it is if you want to walk with me?"

Claire considered leaving with Betty—it would give her more time to ask questions—but the familiar singing compelled her to stay. She'd had a second reason to visit Oakwood, aside from talking to Gordon.

"Could you point to his cottage on a map?" Claire asked.

"I think so." Betty squinted at the map on Claire's phone and said, "It's just off that lane somewhere around there. Now, if you'll excuse me…"

Betty set off weaving through the armchairs while Claire dropped a pin in the middle of the 'somewhere around there' she had pointed to. If reclusive Malcolm had had run-ins with Gordon and Robert, Claire hoped to speak to him next, but first, she had a second bouquet to deliver.

She followed the sound, her footsteps muffled by the plush carpeting. She passed by rooms with open doors, catching glimpses of residents engrossed in their daily routines. The singing grew louder as she approached a room at the end of the hall, the door slightly ajar.

"Who's there?" Mrs Beaton exclaimed, cutting her singing short and squinting towards the door as Claire pushed it open. "*Claire?* Claire Harris? Oh, it *is* you… come in! *Come in…*"

CHAPTER NINE

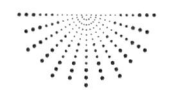

A smile spread across Claire's face as she watched Mrs Beaton arrange the flowers in a vase with great care. Her room was a far cry from the once-cluttered, dilapidated house Claire had visited with Ryan in the cul-de-sac just days ago. Here, the surfaces gleamed, and the air carried a faint scent of lavender.

Sunlight streamed through the large windows, illuminating an array of cuddly cat toys scattered across the bed. Mrs Beaton hummed as she worked, her fingers positioning each stem. Claire's heart swelled with joy at seeing her former neighbour in a clean, well-maintained environment. Her hair looked trimmed and styled, her nightdress a brilliant white, and her skin had taken on a sun-kissed glow.

As Mrs Beaton stepped back to admire her

handiwork, Claire reflected on how little she had known about the woman who had lived next door throughout her childhood. The reclusive Mrs Beaton, with her ever-growing collection of cats and the piles of rubbish that had consumed her life, had always been an enigma.

"Remember this, Mrs Beaton?" Claire said, pulling the scrapbook from her bag.

"Where did you get that?" she hissed, looking around as though Claire had snuck in contraband. "I hid it... that was..."

"In a locked chest in your old house," Claire finished. "You gave it to me before you left. Remember?"

"Hmm."

Mrs Beaton snatched the scrapbook and took it over to the window. She flipped through the pages, her hooked fingers brushing over the pages.

"The best of times," she said. "And the worst of times."

Claire had read every detail in the scrapbook front to back several times, but she listened as Mrs Beaton recounted her remarkable past as though Claire was hearing it with new ears. She spoke of her days as a young opera singer as though recounting a fairy tale, pushed to exhaustion by a relentless mother turned manager who demanded perfection. She recounted the desperate plan to escape her suffocating life by faking her own death, throwing herself overboard, and rowing a lifeboat to shore with the help of a young steward.

"He was a handsome chap," she said, a twinkle in her eye as she brushed her hair from her face. "I asked him to come with me, but he thought I'd lost my marbles. Maybe I had, but he never told my secret. Never told them that Cressida Devey lived."

"And then you moved to Northash," Claire continued the story, "and you started again and had many years of peace."

"I did," Mrs Beaton said, squinting as though she'd forgotten that part. "Are you here to take me home, Claire? Back to the cul-de-sac?"

Claire hesitated, unsure how to respond. Before she could plan a reply, Celia, the nurse, entered the room carrying a small paper cup filled with pills. Mrs Beaton's face twisted into a scowl as the nurse approached, but she accepted the medication and tossed it back with a gulp of water.

"Well done," Celia cried, her tone a little condescending. "Nice to see you have a visitor. Don't forget, it's movie musical night, and we're playing one of your favourites—*Meet Me in St. Louis.*"

Mrs Beaton curled out her bottom lip.

"Never seen it."

"We watched it together just last week. You loved it! You couldn't stop singing that damn Trolley Song. *Clang, clang, clang went the trolley…*"

"*Ding, ding, ding went the bell,*" Mrs Beaton continued.

"Zing, zing, zing went my heartstrings."

"From the moment I saw him, I fell." Celia planted her clenched fists on her hips and stared down at Mrs Beaton like she was addressing a baby. "See! I told you it was one of your favourites."

"I *told* you—I've *never* seen it!"

"Do you even know what film we're talking about?"

She ushered Claire closer with a finger and said, "She thinks I'm stupid, but I know. I know she's working for my mother."

"Not this again…"

Celia sighed and left the room, and as soon as the door closed behind her, Mrs Beaton clenched Claire's arm.

"She's trying to poison me, Claire," she whispered.

Claire's heart sank as she realised that despite the improved living conditions and care, Mrs Beaton's mind still travelled in loops that made little sense. She guided her to sit beside her on the edge of the bed, taking her hand in a comforting gesture.

"No one is trying to poison you, Mrs Beaton," Claire assured her, keeping her voice soft. "The nurses are here to help you, to make sure you're healthy and happy."

Mrs Beaton's eyes widened, a flicker of hope dancing within them.

"Have you come to take me home, Claire?"

Claire's heart clenched at the question. She knew she

couldn't give Mrs Beaton the answer she longed for. She reached out and took her hand in her own. Her skin was leathery, her bones stiff, but the familiarity comforted Claire. She'd missed these hands.

"This is your home now, Mrs Beaton. Oakwood is where you can receive the care and attention you need."

Mrs Beaton grumbled deep in her throat. Claire sought to lift her spirits, eager to share the news about her potential move.

"I visited your old house the other day, Mrs Beaton," Claire said. "The place is doing fine. In fact, if I'm lucky, I might be moving in myself if the mortgage process goes well."

At this, Mrs Beaton's face lit up, the fog of confusion lifting from her eyes.

"Oh, that would be wonderful, Claire! It'll make the perfect house for you and Ryan." A wistful smile played on Mrs Beaton's lips as she delved into her memories. "I remember the day Ryan's mum, Paula, moved into the cul-de-sac. She brought me the most beautiful painting as a housewarming gift. I still have it somewhere..."

She glanced around the room, her brows furrowing as she searched for the elusive painting. After a moment, she shrugged, her attention drawn to a small plush cat toy resting on her bedside table. Picking it up, she stroked its soft fur as though it were a real, living creature.

Claire's eyes narrowed as she noticed a tuft of fluffy

grey fur clinging to the sleeve of Mrs Beaton's nightdress. She reached into her bag, pulling out one of the missing posters for Julia's cat, Mowgli.

"Mrs Beaton, have you seen this cat around here?" Claire asked, holding up the poster. "He's been missing, and his owner is very worried about him."

Mrs Beaton squinted at the poster, and after a moment, she shook her head.

"No, dear, I haven't seen that cat."

With a melancholic sigh, Mrs Beaton rose from her seat and made her way to the window. She pushed it open, allowing a gentle breeze to flutter the curtains. Then, to Claire's surprise, Mrs Beaton sang.

Her voice, though aged, had grown in strength since Claire had last heard her. The sound filled the room and spilled out to the gardens below. Claire watched in awe as Mrs Beaton lost herself in the music, her face alight with joy.

Sudden, forceful banging at the door shattered the moment. Mrs Beaton's singing faltered, her voice growing louder as if to drown out the intrusion. Claire hurried to the door, her heart pounding as she heard a man's voice shouting for Mrs Beaton to keep it down.

As Claire opened the door, she found herself face to face with Gordon once again. His face, contorted with anger, softened when he saw Claire.

"Oh, it's you," he said, his voice still gruff. "You know this caterwauling woman?"

Claire glanced back at Mrs Beaton, who had fallen silent, her eyes wide as she glared at the intruder—possibly another of her mother's evil agents. Turning back to Gordon, Claire offered an apologetic smile.

"Mrs Beaton didn't mean to disturb you. She was just enjoying a bit of singing."

He rubbed at his temples and said, "Look, I'm on a *lot* of medication after being poisoned with that foxglove. I need my rest, and I can't deal with her singing day and night, even at the best of times."

Foxglove poisoning?

Claire had seen it before, back in Northash, when a beekeeper had fallen victim to a deadly dose slipped into her tea. The memory sent a chill down her spine. Gordon was lucky to have survived such an ordeal.

"Just... keep it down, okay?" he said, shuffling away. "I need to sleep or they'll be carting me back to the hospital."

Claire closed the door and returned to Mrs Beaton. She attempted to continue the conversation, but she had retreated into herself. She stared out at the gardens below as the afternoon breeze fluttered the curtains, no longer responding to Claire's questions.

As Claire prepared to leave, promising to visit again soon, she noticed Mrs Beaton plucking at the grey fur clinging to her sleeve. The action seemed almost unconscious, a habit born of years spent surrounded by her feline companions.

On one hand, Claire hoped her gut instinct was wrong.

On the other, it would put at ease a certain café-owner.

She placed a missing poster on the edge of the bed, and with a last promise to visit her old neighbour again, Claire stepped out of the room, her mind still turning over the details of Gordon's poisoning.

Nigella the beekeeper hadn't been lucky enough to walk away from her foxglove poisoning to be annoyed by her neighbour. No wonder Claire had known the toxins DI Moyes had mentioned—she'd helped close the case last spring.

Approaching the front desk, Claire offered a smile to the nurses, who were back to gossiping.

"I don't suppose you've seen a cat around the place?"

The two women exchanged puzzled glances before shaking their heads, barely holding back laughter.

"No pets allowed," Celia replied.

Undeterred, Claire pulled out a stack of the missing posters and placed them on the counter.

"If you do spot the cat matching this description, could you please call me?" she pulled the pen from her little black book and scribbled her number on the bottom of one. "I'm Claire."

"We'll keep an eye out and let you know if we find anything."

As Claire turned to leave, she had another question.

"Why... why does she remember me?"

"Just be grateful she does. Granddaughter?"

"Neighbour."

"It's not an exact science," Celia said, shrugging. "Some days, she knows who I am, other days, I might as well be the devil. Long-term memory... routine... familiarity... emotional connection... for whatever reason, you made it through the fog."

Claire nodded, not wanting to question their connection further. She was just glad it was there.

On her way out, she crossed paths with a familiar figure entering the nursing home in a green paramedic uniform—Emily, the paramedic who had treated Gordon on the scene after his poisoning. She wafted past, her sweet, citrusy perfume trailing behind her. The younger receptionist greeted Emily with a knowing smile.

"Go through, Emily. Mr Wicks will be expecting you."

Claire's eyebrows rose at the receptionist's words, wondering if Emily's presence was more than a mere coincidence. As the paramedic disappeared down the hallway, Claire couldn't help but overhear the receptionists' hushed conversation.

"Like I said, much too young for him," Celia remarked, her voice tinged with disapproval. "Gives me the shivers. What is she? Thirty-five?"

"Who knows what she sees in him?"

Celia rubbed her fingers together and said, "Oh, you *know* what."

CLAIRE PULLED UP THE PIN ON HER MAP AS SUDDEN CLOUDS moved in to ruin the sunshine. Malcolm's cottage could be on her way to the village if she took a different route back. The urge to unravel why Betty had suggested she talk to him propelled her forward, her steps quickening as she rerouted herself down a dirt road.

As the first droplets of rain fell from the sky, she quickened her pace towards Malcolm's cottage. The eight-minute walk seemed to stretch on forever as the spring showers intensified, drenching her hair and clothes. By the time she reached the picturesque dwelling, nestled amidst a wild garden bursting with an array of flowers without a fence to contain it, she was soaked.

Claire paused at the gate, drawn to a peculiar sight. Next to the cottage, in stark contrast to the untamed beauty of Malcolm's garden, lay a patch of grass cut to razor-short perfection, reminiscent of the village green.

The strangeness of the manicured lawn stuck out like a sore thumb, raising more questions in Claire's already perplexed mind.

Undeterred by the 'Keep Out' sign, she approached the front door, where a warm glow emanated from within the cottage. She wrapped her knuckles against the weathered wood, hoping to catch Malcolm's attention, but her knocks went unanswered. Undaunted, she called out, her voice carrying over the patter of the rain.

"*Malcolm?* It's Claire... Claire Harris," she called. "We met briefly. I'm on the Northash team. I wanted to ask you a few questions."

Silence greeted her plea, and a twinge of concern tugged at her chest. With members of the bowls team falling victim to mysterious circumstances, she couldn't help but worry about Malcolm's well-being behind the door.

"Just so I know you're not dead, can you tell me to go away?"

"*Go away.*"

The demand came out so firm and sudden, Claire hopped back from the door and decided against asking twice. As she turned to leave, she saw a familiar plant scattered throughout Malcolm's garden.

Foxgloves.

The tall, bell-shaped flowers bobbed in the rain, their vibrant colours warning of the dangerous toxins held behind their surface beauty. Claire's father had been meticulous in removing the poisonous plants from his own garden after the Nigella incident, more for his own peace of mind.

The presence of foxgloves in Malcolm's garden could have been a mere coincidence, a natural occurrence in the wild beauty of the countryside. Yet, the nagging in the pit of Claire's stomach suggested otherwise.

If Malcolm had nothing to hide, why was he hiding?

Back at the B&B, Claire peeled out of her damp clothes and into a dry hoodie and joggers. She settled at the small desk in her room, still reeling from the revelations at Oakwood and Malcolm's cottage as she watched the rain drizzle down the windowpane.

To distract herself, she pulled out her notepad and the fragrances she had brought along, still determined to capture the spirit of the café. The moment she began mixing the scents, the phone rang. Cradling it between her ear and shoulder, Claire answered.

"Hello?"

"Hey, it's Damon," came the familiar voice from the other end. "How's things down south? Thought I'd check in on my favourite boss."

"Not joined the Janet regime, then?" Claire asked, her

attention divided between the conversation and the delicate balance of fragrances before her. "And things are... going south. But I'll tell you later. How are things going at the shop? I want every detail."

"Your dad's been great. Really easy to work with. But your mother... well, she's as you'd expect. Micromanaging *everything*. It's like she doesn't trust me. Like I haven't been working here for almost two years. Oh, and you'll never guess what she said to a customer this morning..."

As Damon vented his frustrations, she put the phone on loudspeaker, set it down on the desk, and let her mind wander while she mixed fragrance drops into a tiny vial from her scribblings.

According to Betty—like her mother at the candle shop—Gordon had been micromanaging the bowls team. A potential motive behind his poisoning?

And then there was Robert, and his apparent determination to take over the leadership. Despite their past friendship, a power struggle had emerged between the two men. Robert had been Gordon's boss... his friend... and the man his wife—if the gossip was to be believed—chose over him.

Was Robert murdered to stop him from assuming Gordon's control of the group? Betty had mentioned Robert wasn't as afraid of Gordon's technology—he'd had a hand in developing in it—but he seemed to be the only one in the group who hadn't objected to Gordon's tinkering, just the way he was going about implementing it. And Claire still didn't know what the technology was and how it could 'modernise' the simple game, especially now that she'd played a few matches.

The question was, who wanted both men dead, and why? Aside from Gordon, none of them had alibis for either the poisoning or the attack on Robert.

She snapped back to attention as Damon's voice filtered through the phone.

"Claire? Are you there?"

"Sorry, Damon," she said, picking up the phone. "Poor signal down here. What were you saying?"

"I said that I'm taking Sally to The Hesketh Arms for dinner and some homebrew, and that I need to go."

"That sounds lovely. I'll leave you to it. Enjoy your evening," Claire said, trying to remember where she'd been before Damon derailed her thoughts.

As she ended the call, Ryan entered the room with Amelia and Hugo in tow. They had spent the day at a local wool museum, and the kids were eager to talk about it, despite having claimed it would be 'boring.' Hugo listed off facts about the hundreds of wool mills that used to dot the Cotswold landscape, while Amelia showed the pictures she had drawn of spinning wheels, announcing her plans to colour them in later.

"Get much done?" Ryan asked after kissing her on the cheek.

Claire wafted the blend of her candle creation under his nose.

"Does this smell like the café to you?"

"It does, but you don't seem convinced."

"I feel like it's missing something," Claire admitted, corking the small vial. She was still processing the information she had gathered throughout the day, but her stomach was demanding attention as well.

"Why don't we grab a bite to eat somewhere in the village?" she suggested, hoping a change of scenery might help clear her head. "What was the name of that restaurant Evelyn mentioned? The something corner?"

CHAPTER TEN

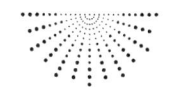

As Mary Todd, the bubbly hostess, led them through the busy restaurant, The Comfy Corner, laughter and conversation filled the air as diners chatted across tables, their voices mingling with the clinking of glasses and the scraping of cutlery against plates. The atmosphere was infectious, and it reminded Claire of The Hesketh Arms back home, albeit with many more tables and a much lower ceiling.

"I can't believe we got a table on such short notice," Ryan said. "This place is packed."

Claire nodded in agreement. She had expected a long wait or perhaps even a polite rejection, given how busy the place had looked through the windows alone. Yet, Mary had greeted them with a beaming smile and maternal warmth that made them feel welcome, insisting a table was already waiting for them.

As they navigated the maze of tables with the children trailing behind, they passed an open archway leading into another tiny room. A familiar group occupied the sole table in the off-shoot room. Claire's step faltered for a moment; she felt Ryan's hand press against the small of her back, urging her forward.

"It's like everyone in the village is here," Claire whispered to Ryan as they weaved in and out of the tables, following Mary, who was keeping a mental log of all the drink orders being barked at her by the locals. "Including what's left of the Peridale bowls team in that separate room."

"You know what they say about the countryside," Ryan said. "I keep catching people staring at us like we're outsiders."

"*We* live in the countryside too, Ryan."

"But not *this* kind of countryside," Ryan replied. "This is like Hobbit land."

"Hobbiton, The Shire," Mary called over her shoulder, without missing a beat of Ryan's low voice. "I've heard people say J. R. R. Tolkien visited the Cotswolds often. He might have been inspired by this very building."

"Meant nothing by it, of course." Ryan's cheeks burned red as he pushed forward a surprised smile. "Seems like a friendly place."

"Oh, it is, but I'd say you're right to be a little suspicious," Mary said, more discreetly, as she showed them to their table at the back of the restaurant. "Folks are mostly decent, but let's just say we've had enough bad eggs these past few years to make an omelette or two. Not that people won't be friendly to your face, mind you." She pulled out some chairs at the table where Greta and Eugene were already seated. "It's what people say behind your back that really stings. Pay it no mind, though. Given what I hear in here daily, none of us are exempt from the gossips of Peridale." She pushed forward a bright smile and said, "I'll give you a minute to catch up on the menu."

Claire and Ryan exchanged glances as Mary left them to settle in. Claire was accustomed to gossip and stories, but Ryan might have had a point about Northash not being as 'countryside' as Peridale. Like Mary in the restaurant, Claire picked up much of the gossip in her candle shop. She had been the centre of a few wild stories herself, but at least back home she was familiar with the faces the darting eyes belonged to.

"People *are* staring," Claire muttered, trying to focus on the extensive menu.

"So, you've noticed too?" Greta remarked, peering over the menu and speaking at a volume that could have been overheard by at least half the restaurant. "There's a rumour going around that one of us..." She glanced at

Amelia and Hugo as they stared at her instead of the menus Mary had just put in front of them. "...one of us took Gordon out of the competition. And by one of us, I mean *me*."

"Is that the guy that almost died?" Hugo asked.

Ryan nodded, patting him on the shoulder and tapping the menu in front of him to refocus his attention.

"I *told* you something bad was going to happen," Amelia said. "Evelyn said I have a gift."

"Mad as a box of frogs, isn't she?" Eugene commented, a little too giddily. "I love her eccentric ways, but I couldn't stand the thought of another one of her dry nut roasts, and I'm married to a vegan."

"We thought you might feel the same, so we reserved you some seats," Greta explained. "People haven't stopped staring since we walked in."

"The attention is rather fabulous, wouldn't you say?"

"Spoken like a true politician, Eugene," Greta said.

"*Former* mayor," he corrected, "and I prefer 'actor' these days. You saw the review of my spectacular turn as Mother Superior in *Sister Act*, didn't you? The *Northash Observer* called it the most 'audacious' performance Northash has ever seen."

"I thought you were doing *Fiddler on the Roof*?"

"It's a rotating production. One night on, one night off. We're trying to appeal to more markets to get bums on seats, which you'd *know* if you ever came to one of my performances."

"I can't stand the theatre," Greta said. "You always get a better view on the TV."

"I didn't even know Northash had a theatre," Ryan commented.

"Technically outside, but close enough," Eugene said, his eyes widening as he nodded at something across the restaurant. "But who needs actors when the local drama unfolding before us is as juicy as this..."

Claire twisted in her seat as the restaurant silenced. By the door, Gordon clung to a cane while absorbing the muttering and shocked faces turning his way. He offered a tight smile and a nod to a few people before ducking into the private room. The mumbling turned to full-blown talking, then shouting. Claire wished they would all quieten down so she could hear what was going on in the other room.

"Five pounds on it all kicking off," Eugene said.

"Tenner," Greta replied, holding out her hand for Eugene to shake. "You should have heard them when I was waiting for our drinks at the bar. They were all squabbling about who was going to be the next leader. Gordon somehow survived his poisoning, and Robert has been dead for five minutes, and all they seem to care about was who should get the crown."

Claire remembered her conversation with Damon

earlier and her suspicions that the poisoning and the murder had been linked by a scramble for leadership.

"I think we're doing fine without a leader," Eugene announced. "We're like a cast."

"I thought *I* was the leader?" Greta arched an eyebrow. "And where's that smiley woman? I want to order some food this side of midnight."

"Well, I suppose you could be the leader," Eugene grumbled, adjusting his ruffly collared shirt. "You did rather take charge today, not that we voted on it."

"*Someone* had to pull us together. No offence, Claire and Ryan," Greta whispered, and Claire and Ryan exchanged guilty glances. "And Mary's over there eavesdropping by that archway."

"I'm jealous," Eugene admitted. "I bet she's getting all the good gossip."

Claire was jealous too, but she was glad Eugene was the one brave enough to admit it aloud.

"Forget the other team for a moment," Greta insisted, leaning into the table. "We have to focus on strategy if *we* want to win. We slipped through by the skin of our teeth today. All the teams have agreed that we'll let things cool off for a few days before we restart the tournament, which gives us extra time to scrub up on your moves, Claire."

"It was Claire *and* Ryan before, Gran."

"Ryan picked it up faster than you," Greta said with a

soft sigh. "I know us Harris women aren't the most athletic, and you rolled the winning blow—okay, 'blow' wasn't the best choice of words given what happened to Robert, and—Ah! Mary. We're ready to order if you've got a minute?"

As Mary talked them all into ordering the 'house special'—something called a Peridale Pie—Claire twisted in her seat at the sound of a door slamming. Betty stood in the archway, and the silence that followed made Claire assume she had just missed Gordon's exit.

"Nothing like a murder to get folks riled up," Mary said, rolling her eyes as she stabbed her notepad with her pen after finishing scribbling down their orders. "The sooner someone catches whoever is behind that bashing, the better."

Mary left, and despite her words being as blunt as the blow that took Robert out, Claire agreed. And she was itching to know what she had just missed by not being a fly on the wall in that dining room.

"You'll be the one to solve it, Claire," Eugene proclaimed. "Everyone in Northash knows you're good at this sort of thing. You inherited your father's talents."

"I'll toast to that," Greta said, lifting her whisky glass before taking a sharp sip. "So, did you track down Betty today?"

Claire leaned in, her voice low as she revealed the events that had unfolded at the nursing home. She recounted her conversations with Betty and Gordon, the visit to Mrs Beaton, and the discovery of the poison's identity. Eugene's eyes widened as he made the same connection Claire had, recalling the beekeeper who had been poisoned at the garden centre back home. Greta gasped when Claire mentioned Gordon's relationship with the paramedic from the scene.

"She's young for him," she exclaimed, shaking her head. "But I'm not surprised to learn about Gordon and Betty being separated. They have a strange chemistry, the kind that only comes from tolerating someone you once loved."

Eugene nodded in agreement. "Everyone on the team seems like that, at least around Gordon. Did you notice how much lighter they were at the tournament without him there?"

In the background, the members of the Peridale bowls team left the private room one by one. Betty maintained a smile as she walked through the pub, as if trying to hide the obvious tension caused by their group's presence. Malcolm, his head bowed, rushed to the door first, avoiding every eye in the room. Henry, on the other hand, propped himself up at the bar while Betty followed Malcolm out with a more measured pace.

"Peridale Pies!" Mary announced, hurrying to their table with plates stacked up her arms. "Fresh out of the oven, so be careful. Who ordered theirs with gravy?"

Claire lifted a finger, and Mary reached across the table, sloshing the gravy into Claire's lap. "Oh, dear. I'm so sorry! I don't know what's got into me today. All this drama has my nerves unsteady. Let me grab you a cloth."

"It's fine," Claire said, trying to smile away the awkwardness as she dabbed at it with a napkin. "I'll see if I can sort it out in the bathroom."

"That door over there," Mary directed.

Still dabbing at the puddle of gravy on her favourite vintage Spice Girls t-shirt, Claire pushed into the women's bathroom and approached the sink. Barely tall enough, she managed to run the t-shirt under the tap. She went to pump the hand soap, but a blast of air hit her palm instead—empty.

"Great," Claire muttered to herself. "So now I'm wet *and* covered in gravy."

From behind a cubicle door came the unmistakable sound of muffled weeping. Someone was having a worse day than Claire and her t-shirt. She turned off the tap and listened closely.

"Are you okay?" Claire asked, her knuckles poised inches from the wooden door.

The crying stopped, and after a brief pause, the toilet flushed, and the lock clicked open. The door swung ajar, revealing Julia patting her eyes, now bare of makeup. Observing her in this state, adorned in mascara and lipstick—contrasting sharply with her usually bare-faced look—and clad in a body-skimming vintage dress, Claire couldn't help but think Julia looked like an old Hollywood star, if not for the tears.

"I'd recognise that Northern accent anywhere," Julia said, forcing out a laugh as she stepped out.

"I do sound rather common in comparison."

"I like it," Julia said, reaching into her handbag to pull out a small packet of wet wipes at the sight of Claire's stain. She held them out. "It sounds honest."

"We might be too honest sometimes," Claire said, peeling back the wet wipes to dab at the fabric.

"I wish some people around here were more honest."

"Is that about someone in particular?"

Julia sighed. "My gran. She wouldn't tell me where she was at the time of Robert's murder. I asked her again today, and she said she was planning a surprise for her husband's birthday. It is his birthday next week, but I felt like she was lying to me."

"Would she?"

Julia shrugged.

"Is that why you're upset?"

"Oh, no." She wiped away the mascara dribbling from her lower lashes in the mirror. "Someone called about Mowgli earlier. They said they'd found a cat in their conservatory and they were certain he was the cat on the missing poster. I rushed over, but it wasn't Mowgli." She clenched her eyes, and another tear squeezed out. Claire pulled a fresh blue tissue from the dispenser and handed it over. "I know it's silly. He's just a cat… but… we've been through a lot over the years."

"It's not silly," Claire replied, their eyes meeting in the mirror. "My cats have seen me at my absolute worst. I'd feel the same if I couldn't find one of them."

Claire pulled out her phone, scrolling through her gallery until she found a rare photo of the two felines sitting side by side, their eyes fixed on the camera with an almost regal air. She thought about their last goodbye that morning, but she missed them.

"They're beautiful."

"My two troublemakers," Claire said. "Domino and Sid. Sid's a total couch potato, like me, but if any of them were to go wandering, I'd put my money on Domino."

"I should be out looking for him, but my husband—bless him—thought coming here would cheer me up before we go looking again. It usually works. We had our first date here." A hint of a smile lifted her lips. "It's difficult to be distracted tonight. The atmosphere is as thick as buttercream in there."

"You noticed it too?"

"It's the Peridale bowls team," Julia explained with a hint of apology in her voice. "But like everyone else, I can't stop thinking about what happened to Robert. And not just how horrible it was, but what led them there. *How* did it get to that point?"

"I'm not alone there, either," Claire said, lowering her voice. "Listen, I've been hoping to pick your brains after you made that timeline in your notebook. I talked to Betty and Gordon, and I think—"

The bathroom door burst open, and Dot hurried in.

"Ah, Julia! There you are. I was on my way out when I noticed Barker alone at your table and he said you'd been gone at least fifteen minutes. He sent me in to make sure you hadn't done a runner through the bathroom window." Dot sent a sharp glance at Claire. "Is this your doing? Are you accusing Julia like your horrible grandmother just accused me as I was passing her table?"

"If you think *she's* horrible, meet my other gran."

"Claire wasn't accusing me of anything," Julia said. "She was just making sure I was alright. I couldn't hold back the tears."

"Oh." Dot nodded, not needing to ask why Julia would be crying. "Mowgli will turn up, love. Not to sound like Evelyn, but that phone call earlier is a sign that people are keeping an eye out for him. Those posters will bring him back home. He won't have gone far." She glanced at Claire with eyes like slits before turning back to Julia. "I need to talk to you about something sensitive. Alone. I know you said you're not up to your old snooping ways, but things have taken a turn."

"You can say it now, Gran."

Claire appreciated the vote of confidence, even if Dot gave her another distrusting glare.

"Gordon is accusing one of *our* team of poisoning him," Dot revealed with a deep sigh. "*And* he thinks one of us murdered Robert. Gordon just tried to fire us all from the bowls team, but we… well… we all stood up for ourselves. He stormed out before we could oust him, but that's where things are heading. With any luck, they'll let me take charge so I can put things right. But if Gordon is right… if one of the team killed Robert… I might need your help, Julia. Any of us could be next."

"I'll do what I can," Julia said, though she didn't seem sure. "Where were you when Robert was hit, Gran?"

"I already told you," Dot said with an airy wave of her hand. "I was planning a surprise for Percy's birthday. It's next week, you know. Now, best to get back to Barker before he thinks I've joined you out of the window."

Julia sighed, but she nodded and didn't push the topic further. She seemed too exhausted, but even Claire, who didn't know Dot, noticed a warble in her voice that made her sure tone sound like she was lying.

"Thank you," Claire said, holding out the wet wipes.

"Keep them," she said as she pulled open the door. "I've got a two-year-old, so I never leave the house without at least a couple of packets."

"How…" the door swung shut behind Dot, who fired one last distrusting glance at Claire. "…resourceful."

Claire hoped she could pick Julia's brain tomorrow.

Not only was she related to an obvious suspect, but her café was also at the centre of the village. And given that list, Julia was a woman who was paying attention.

After drying off the almost faded stain thanks to the wet wipes, Claire returned to the table where Greta and Eugene were digging through their pies. She scanned the restaurant for Julia and her husband, but they were already on their way to the door.

"It sort of tastes like a little of everything," Greta said, moving her fork around the pie's innards. "It's not unpleasant, but…"

"It's almost like it's been curried," Eugene added, wrinkling his nose as he forked some into his mouth. "It's passable, but what's wrong with a simple meat and potato? Cheese and onion, even? You're right, Ryan. We are *deep* in the countryside here."

Claire took a bite of her Peridale Pie, the unique blend of flavours dancing on her tongue. It was an unusual combination, but like Greta said, not unpleasant.

As the evening wore on, the atmosphere in the pub settled into a more relaxed rhythm. The earlier commotion seemed to dissipate as patrons focused on their meals and conversations. When the time came for dessert, they all opted for the salted caramel cheesecake. The rich texture and the perfect balance of sweet and salty made for a delicious end to the meal. As they savoured the last bites, Claire felt a sense of contentment wash over her, grateful for the brief respite from the day's chaos.

With their appetites satisfied and spirits lifted, they bid farewell to Mary, who enveloped them in warm hugs before they departed. As they stepped out into the night, Claire noticed the library across the street, a building she hadn't noticed on her way in.

Through the library's large windows, Claire spotted Julia and Dot chatting with the woman Jessie had called 'Sue' in the café earlier that day. Standing next to Julia, the resemblance was undeniable—she had to be Julia's younger sister.

"I overheard something strange in the bathroom," Claire said to Greta and Eugene when Ryan walked ahead to keep up with the kids, who'd bounced off into the night with unnatural amounts of energy after the rich dessert. "Gordon is pointing the finger at his teammates, and they're on the brink of kicking him out."

"*See!*" Eugene said, patting Claire's shoulder. "Not only are you an expert at sniffing these crumbs out, but you're already looking in the right direction."

"I still reckon it was *her*," Greta said, jerking her head towards the library as they walked up the street. "I still don't trust her."

"I don't think she's a cold-blooded killer," Claire said,

"but Julia doesn't seem to trust her either. She thinks her gran is lying about her alibi."

"*Ah ha*! Why would she lie about her alibi if she's innocent?"

As they walked back to the B&B under the glow of the moon on a cloudless night, Claire knew her gran had a point. Something to dig into, not that Dot would be forthcoming with her after how she'd glared at her in the bathroom, especially if she was withholding from Julia.

There were still members of the team Claire hadn't spoken to, and as she snuggled into bed, she looked at the pin on her map. Tomorrow, she'd complete the set and speak to Malcolm and Henry. The two men might have been quiet and reserved, but they'd been present as much as everyone else, always watching from the side-lines.

"What's on your mind?" Ryan asked as he settled in next to her.

"Nothing particular tonight," she said, snuggling closer. "But tomorrow, I need to speak to Malcolm and Henry."

"They seem quiet."

"Precisely," she said, letting her heavy lids close. "Which only makes me wonder, what aren't they saying?"

CHAPTER ELEVEN

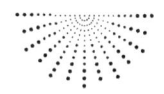

The next morning, Greta and Eugene tried their best to train Claire and Ryan, but their efforts were somewhat hampered by the constant speculation about Robert's murder that seemed to permeate every corner of the green.

Earlier that morning, Claire had stopped by the packed café to grab a coffee, where the air was thick with theories and gossip. Many people thought Betty was behind both, with reports of the blood on her hands at the scene exaggerated to people swearing they'd seen her clutching a bloody bowl. Others suggested Robert had poisoned Gordon before taking his own life out of guilt. And Dot made sure to remind everyone that 'the leader of the Northash team' had been missing from the green around the time of the murder.

Julia remained impartial, speaking only when spoken to and revealing little. Claire could see the gears turning in her mind, but the woman was far too busy running about the place to share her theories, spinning every plate while her sister tried to keep up. Claire still wanted to pick her brains, but she'd have to catch her when the café wasn't as busy.

Claire focused on her bowling technique as Greta offered pointers. She was lining up her next shot when Eugene let out a dramatic yelp after he threw his bowl. He clutched his wrist, his face contorted in exaggerated pain.

"My wrist!" he cried. "It's *broken!*"

"Honestly, Eugene. There's no need for theatrics at every given opportunity." Greta examined his hand, twisting it like she was wringing out a cloth. "It's likely just a sprain, but I'll take you to the hospital to get it checked."

Eugene continued moaning like the cowardly lion while Greta took his good arm and helped him to his feet.

"They'll have to amputate," he announced. "I'll only be able to play one-handed characters from now on."

"And a fine hook-handed pirate you'd make, but it won't come to that," Greta said, helping Eugene limp along to the edge of the green as though he'd broken both ankles too. "You two keep practising. It should only take the doctors a few minutes to chop his hand off."

Claire watched them go, stifling a smile. She turned to see Ryan observing a very bored-looking Amelia and Hugo. Neither of them had moved from the bench in front of the café all morning.

"What do you say we head over to that indoor play area we passed on the drive here?" Ryan suggested. "Looks like it could be fun."

The kids' eyes lit up at the promise of something more exciting than bowls. They quickly gathered their things, ready to leave.

"You go ahead," Claire said, her mind already drifting to the next step in her investigation. "I'll meet you there later if I can, but first, I need to see a man about a bowl."

Ryan gave her a knowing look, understanding that her curiosity about the case was far from satisfied. With a nod, he gathered up the kids and set off, leaving Claire to her own devices.

She followed the pin on her map out of the village, returning to Malcolm's cottage on its solitary country lane far off on the outskirts. This time, there was no denying he was at home. Malcolm knelt in front of his cottage, his hands deep in the soil as he tended to his garden. Beside him, Henry sat on an upturned plant pot, sipping tea in his red postal uniform. The scene reminded Claire of herself and her father, and a pang of homesickness hit her.

Henry spotted her approach. He cleared his throat,

and the laughter and smiles vanished from both men's faces. Malcolm stood up, removing his gloves with deliberate care.

"You were here yesterday too," he stated, his tone flat and unwelcoming.

Claire nodded, maintaining a friendly manner despite the chilly reception.

"I just want to talk," she explained, keeping her voice light. "I'm trying to figure out what's going on." She hesitated, deciding not to mention that Betty had suggested Claire speak to him. "I want the tournament to resume so we can get on with winning."

She forced a laugh, hoping to break the tension, and Henry chuckled, amused by her competitive spirit. Malcolm remained stoic, his surly expression devoid of a lick of humour. He regarded Claire with a cold, assessing stare, as if trying to discern her true motives.

Claire watched as Henry muttered something to Malcolm, prompting the surly man to step aside, allowing her to enter the garden. She took a moment to admire the lush greenery surrounding her.

"Your garden is lovely," Claire complimented, scanning the various plants. "Delphiniums, and next to them, the soft pink blooms are astilbes? They do well in the shade."

"You know your stuff," Malcolm remarked, arching a suspicious brow.

"My father is a keen gardener. He'd be impressed by your handiwork." She took a step closer to the flower bed Malcolm had been working on, her trainers crunching on the gravel path. "And we can't forget the foxgloves. They're just starting to open up over there." She gestured towards a cluster of tall spikes adorned with bell-shaped flowers, ranging from deep purples to soft pinks. "Bees love them, though they can be quite poisonous to other animals, can't they? People, too."

Malcolm folded his arms tightly across his chest.

"So? They're all over the village this time of year."

An awkward silence swept through the garden on the breeze, and Claire sensed that both men had a lot left unsaid, bubbling just beneath the surface. Henry offered Claire his plant pot, which she accepted gratefully. Sensing a golden opportunity to get both men talking, Claire offered her condolences for what had happened to Gordon and Robert. To her surprise, neither man seemed particularly upset by the recent events.

"Given Gordon and Robert's ways," Henry said, sipping his tea, "I'm only surprised something hadn't happened sooner." He quickly added, "I wouldn't wish death on anyone, of course."

"Of course," Claire repeated. "Who would?" She paused, and added, "Well, I suppose the person who hit Robert over the head did."

An awkward silence followed, disturbed only by Henry's slurps.

"My gran can be a little controlling with our team," Claire said, sensing a way in. "Is that what you mean by their 'ways'?"

Claire watched as Malcolm's expression shifted, a flicker of discomfort crossing his weathered features. The older man cleared his throat, his gaze drifting to the vibrant flowers that surrounded them.

"Gordon, well, he was always a bit... particular about the way things were done," Malcolm began. "Liked to have everything under *his* control, you know?"

Claire nodded, sensing that Malcolm was warming up to the conversation. She had questions, but she held back, giving him space to talk.

"And Robert, he was cut from the same cloth," Malcolm continued. "Always had to have things *his* way. Butted heads with Gordon a lot, especially when it came to the team. They used to be friends, but things spoiled after…" He cleared his throat. "Well, that's none of my business."

"Betty told me that Gordon and Robert used to work together," Claire pushed. "What was that like?"

"They were thick as thieves, until…" He trailed off, a muscle in his jaw twitching. "Like I said, none of my business."

"Until the affair?" Claire prompted.

"Exactly that," Henry said. "Betty and Robert were having it off for years, right under Gordon's nose."

Claire's eyes widened at the revelation. "And he never noticed?"

"Gordon was always *laser*-focused on his work," Malcolm continued. "He worked in a rather large factory that made lasers for all sorts of things—supermarket tills, car systems, you name it. Robert was promoted above Gordon, but he was never as devoted to the job. All his free time left him plenty of time to sneak around with Betty behind Gordon's back, that's for sure."

"That can't have been easy for Gordon to find out about."

"Gordon only retired once he found out about the affair," Henry said, his tone tinged with a hint of sympathy. "I think he hoped he'd be promoted all the way to the top one day. He's a very goal-oriented man. Like Malcolm said, laser focused. But the affair must have crushed him. In true British fashion, he kept calm and carried on."

"That's when Gordon became obsessed with focusing on the team and pushed everyone away," Malcolm added gruffly. "Gave him something to focus on, I suppose."

"But that didn't go over well with the rest of you, did it?"

Henry and Malcolm exchanged a glance.

"I've always thought Malcolm should be the leader,"

Henry admitted. "He's calm, level-headed, and does a fine job leading the Peridale Green Fingers gardening group."

A flush crept up Malcolm's neck, and he shifted his weight from one foot to the other, clearly uncomfortable with the compliment.

"I don't *want* to lead the group," he muttered, his gaze fixed on the vibrant blooms surrounding them. "And to be honest, I've been on the verge of leaving for months. This tournament was to be my final one."

Claire's eyes widened at this revelation. "Why is that?"

"After what Gordon has been doing to me," he began, his voice low and measured, "I was ready to quit."

"Controlling the team?"

"Controlling my garden." He jerked his head at the strange patch of short grass Claire had noticed on her first visit. "He bought the plot for cheap from the farmer who owns the surrounding land. He's been talking about buying a dedicated training pitch for years. I just didn't think he'd buy the patch next door."

"He wants to entice the *youth*," Henry grumbled. "He thought that by using technology to 'update' the game, he could attract a younger crowd. Lasers for training, technology in the bowls to speed them up... Silly ideas that take away from the essence of the sport. It's fine as it is. It's supposed to be a genteel game for the retired. We don't need a fancy ground, lasers, or youths. The green's always been fine, and there'll always be retired people to play."

"Gordon's been going through the council to have my garden destroyed because it overlaps with his precious patch," Malcolm said, glancing at the short grass out of the corner of his eye. "I've been left in peace here for years until Gordon, and I won't get rid of my garden for anyone or anything. He could have bought land *anywhere…*"

As Malcolm's temper flared, Henry cleared his throat, a gentle reminder for his friend to rein in his emotions. Malcolm took a deep breath as Henry drained the last of his tea and set the cup down on the doorstep.

"I need to get on with my rounds," he said, giving Malcolm a nod. "Can't have the post being late, even with all this excitement."

As Henry left, Malcolm closed up again, making it clear that Claire was no longer welcome. Before she could leave, however, a pressing question lingered in her mind.

"If a member of your team killed Robert and poisoned Gordon," Claire asked, her voice steady, "who would you say it was?"

"There's only one woman in the middle of both of them, and her fancy new apartment didn't come cheap."

Claire's brow furrowed. "What do you mean by that?"

"Gossip around the village is that Betty made her way

into Gordon *and* Robert's wills," Malcolm said. "Take from that what you will."

Claire almost mentioned that Betty had pointed the finger at Malcolm, but she held her tongue, not wanting to push her luck—or his temper. If the gossip about Betty being in both of the victims' wills happened to be true, he'd given her some good information to dig into. She thanked Malcolm for his time and turned to leave. As she made her way across the garden, Claire's foot caught on something hard poking out between the gravel and the flowerbeds. It felt like a stone, but smoother and rounded. She bent down to get a better look when her phone rang.

Claire hesitated, thinking it might be a scam call, but the local area code matched that of the B&B. Curious, she answered.

"Hello?"

"Is this Claire?" a female voice inquired on the other end.

"Speaking. Who's this?"

"You were at Oakwood the other day?" It was Celia, the older receptionist from the nursing home. "I think you should come right away."

CHAPTER TWELVE

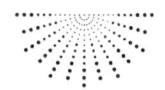

"We caught her red-handed!" Celia explained as Claire hurried after her down the corridors at Oakwood. "She was sneaking chicken from the kitchen. One of the porters followed her and discovered something quite strange... even by Mrs Beaton's standards."

They turned a corner, and the nurse led Claire down a narrow staircase towards the cellar. The air grew cooler as they descended into the scent of musty dampness mingled with the faint, unmistakable tang of cat litter.

"She set the whole thing up herself," she continued, pushing open a heavy wooden door. "I don't know what possessed her."

"It's her default setting."

Claire stepped into the cellar, her eyes adjusting to the

dim light. There, in the corner, a makeshift cat bed, complete with a litter tray and a bowl of water. A half-eaten chicken carcass lay near a blanket. Claire crouched, running her fingers over a few tufts of grey fur, the same soft texture as the hair she'd noticed on Mrs Beaton's nightdress.

"Thank you for calling me," Claire breathed, her heart skipping a beat. "I think this is him."

"I've worked here coming on twenty-two years," she said, letting out a strained, bemused laugh. "Stealing food and harbouring a cat? That's a new one."

"Like I said—"

"Default setting," Celia interrupted. "You mean to tell me she used to go around *catnapping?*"

"Exactly, but for what it's worth, I doubt she knows she's stealing anything." Claire dusted off her knees as she looked around the cellar for any signs of feline eyes glowing in the dark. "Where's Mrs Beaton now?"

"She became quite agitated when confronted and she scurried off before anyone could get any answers from her." Celia yanked open the cellar door, letting in the fresh air from upstairs. "As for the cat, he bolted as soon as he saw daylight. He could be anywhere by now."

Still missing.

"There's a search party scouring the place as we speak. We can't have a cat running loose. It's against the rules."

Claire joined in the search, eyes peeled for any sign of

a fluffy tail swishing about the place. She checked under tables, behind curtains, and in every nook and cranny she could find in the lounge area. The residents, busy watching TV, seemed oblivious to the feline fugitive. A man, his attention briefly diverted from a solitary one-sided game of chess, pointed down a hallway.

"If you're looking for the Wailing Woman, she went that way."

Claire thanked him and hurried down the corridor. As she passed the open door next to Mrs Beaton's bedroom, familiar voices caught her attention. Through the crack, she spotted Betty and Gordon. Their backs were to her as they stared out of the large window, nothing more than shadows as the afternoon sun washed out the room.

"Don't *push* me, Gordon," Betty hissed. "You will not keep controlling me like this."

"Controlling *you*?" he scoffed. "Tell them my 'big secret', Betty. This is looking far worse for you."

"I didn't do—"

"You were *seen* picking those foxgloves."

"And they went straight into a vase!" she cried. "You know how much I've always loved those flowers."

"Yes, I do." He sighed, turning to her. "I should have known you were behind this. You were so *quick* to replace me. You'd be happy to get rid of me."

"Gordon, I—"

"You'll what?" he snapped. "Find another of my friends to shack up with? Good luck. I don't have many left."

"And I wonder why. It wasn't like that."

"You're a scarlet woman, Betty Fletcher. I rue the day I ever met—"

In a flash of fury, Betty's hand connected with Gordon's cheek, the sharp slap echoing in the room. Claire flinched, her breath catching in her throat. She backed away from the door and spun around, startled by an unexpected tap on her shoulder. She found herself face to face with DI Moyes.

"Detective, I was just…" Claire gestured to the room. "I was just passing by."

"It looks like it," she replied, concealing a smile that let Claire know Moyes had been standing there watching her for some time. "If you wouldn't mind stepping aside, I'm here to talk to Gordon. There are some interesting rumours about his ex-wife that I need to clarify."

"Is this about Betty being in Gordon's and Robert's wills?"

The DI's cool smile flickered. She remained tight-lipped, her silence speaking volumes. Claire had hit a nerve, and the detective seemed both irritated and impressed that Claire had beaten her to the punch.

"I'm not here for that," Claire clarified. "I'm looking for Julia's missing cat."

"Cat?" the DI echoed, her brow furrowing. "I just saw some old woman sneaking off into the garden clutching a cat."

Claire's heart leapt, a surge of hope coursing through her.

"A *grey* cat?"

She shrugged. "Possibly."

Betty chose that moment to storm out of Gordon's room, her face flushed as red as the carpet. The DI held up a hand, stopping her in her tracks.

"Don't go anywhere," Moyes warned. "I need to talk to you. Whether we do it here or at the station is your choice."

Claire itched to stay, but the thought of Mowgli being within reach pushed her forward. The mystery of Betty and the wills would have to wait—she had to find that cat.

She hurried back through the lounge, eliciting groans as she flew by the TV screen. The patio doors were open, letting in the afternoon air. She stood blinded for a moment and listened to the grunts of the ongoing tennis game as her eyes adjusted.

Then she heard it.

Singing.

She crossed the manicured lawn, passing by a small group of residents playing bowls next to the tennis courts. The singing grew louder as she approached an ivy-covered pergola hidden between swaying trees, their white and pink blossom lit up by the high noon sunshine.

There, sitting cross-legged on the white wood of the pergola, was Mrs Beaton. In her arms, she cradled a fluffy grey cat, stroking its fur as she sang a soothing song. Mowgli's eyes were closed as he purred, rubbing his face against Mrs Beaton's fingers.

Claire slowed her approach, not wanting to startle them. Mrs Beaton continued singing, lost in her own world. The notes weren't perfect, her instrument scratchy, but the sound had a haunting beauty that made the hairs on Claire's arm stand to attention. Mrs Beaton circled around the same few lines until her energy seemed to vanish. When the melody drifted away to a hum, Claire cleared her throat.

"Mrs Beaton?"

Her eyes opened, squinting up in recognition.

"*Claire?* Lovely afternoon we're having." She looked down at Mowgli, running her hand from the top of his head to the tip of his tail. "They're trying to take her off me. They're trying to take Molly away. I bet my mother put them up to this."

Claire approached Mrs Beaton, her heart aching for the confused woman. She crouched next to her, catching Mowgli's attention. He looked with wide green eyes—the missing poster hadn't done his majestic beauty justice.

"You love cats, don't you?"

"More than anything."

"Molly was your first."

"She's such a good girl."

"Do you remember what Molly looked like?"

"Of course." Mrs Beaton glared at her. "She had fur as red as the heat of a fire, and…"

Mrs Beaton's wrinkled brow scrunched, her eyes clouding with uncertainty as she looked down at the cat in her lap.

"You sent me on a wild goose chase looking for Molly once," Claire continued, a slight smile tugging at her lips. "Back at the cul-de-sac, remember? I ended up falling down the entrance to a tunnel. Almost broke my neck."

As Claire spoke, the tension in Mrs Beaton's shoulders eased. The fog of confusion lifted from her eyes.

"There was a woman in my garden."

Claire smiled, despite the memory not being a pleasant one. The woman in Mrs Beaton's garden had been dead—murdered by a former rival—and the investigation over the following weeks led to it being decided that Mrs Beaton couldn't live on her own anymore.

"You were always such a helpful girl, Claire. Always ready to lend a hand."

Claire smiled, relieved to see Mrs Beaton's mind

clearing. She reached out and stroked the cat's soft fur, as soft as butter.

"This cat isn't Molly, Mrs Beaton," Claire dared. "He's been missing for a few days now."

Claire pulled out the missing poster from her back pocket, the image of the grey cat staring back at them.

"This cat is a boy, and his name is Mowgli," she explained, and at the mention of his name, Mowgli let out a soft meow. "His mother is missing him terribly. She's been quite upset since he disappeared." Mrs Beaton's gaze flickered between the poster and the cat in her arms. "I'm sure she'll be over the moon to hear that you found him."

Mrs Beaton's grip on Mowgli loosened, and Claire seized the opportunity to scoop him up. He was a big boy, as heavy as a newborn settling against her chest. Mowgli wrapped his paws around her shoulder, his claws digging into her t-shirt as he clung to her. She was sure he'd drawn blood, but she didn't dare move him in case he bolted again.

"Should we go back inside?" Claire said, standing up and holding out a helping hand. "I think it's almost lunchtime."

Mrs Beaton nodded, and Claire helped her to her feet before guiding her back to the nursing home. Some of the nurses and residents shook their heads at Mrs

Beaton, but she didn't seem to notice. She slumped down in a chair by the TV playing *Cash in the Attic*.

"I don't know what we're going to do with her," Celia muttered as Claire walked past. "What will it be next?"

Claire wasn't sure, but she also wasn't sure how long Mowgli would let her carry him. She left the nursing home, and—for now—the cat seemed content, his purrs vibrating against her chest as she walked.

As she made her way down the long, winding driveway, Claire considered calling Julia to share the good news. Her fingers itched to dial the number, but curiosity held her back. She wanted to see for herself just how far Mrs Beaton had gone to take Mowgli.

Julia had mentioned living near Peridale Farm, and a quick one-handed check of her phone revealed only three houses on that lane. The vintage car would be hard to miss.

Claire set off towards the farm, a spring in her step despite the grey clouds gathering on the horizon.

"Your mum's going to be so happy to see you," she said, scratching behind his ears. "She's been worried sick, you know."

AS THEY NEARED THE FRONT DOOR, MOWGLI RECOGNISED his surroundings, and there was nothing Claire could do to fight his wriggling. They were both soaked through from the sudden downpour that had started halfway across the fields of Peridale Farm. He bounced across the garden and scrambled through the open front window.

Home at last.

"*Mowgi!*" a little girl cried, missing out the 'l'.

A scream of delight followed, and a smile tugged at Claire's lips at the thought of the reunion taking place inside. She was about to turn and leave, content to let the family have their moment, when the front door flung open.

"Claire…?"

"I found him," she explained, hunched as the rain pelted down around her. "It's a long story."

Before she could say more, Julia rushed into the rain and grabbed Claire in a tight hug. They both laughed, despite being soaked to the bone.

"Come inside," Julia insisted, pulling back to look at Claire. "You're in luck. The fire just got going."

Claire hesitated for a moment, not wanting to impose. But the thought of warming up by a fire was too tempting to resist.

As she stepped inside, the homely atmosphere warmed her through. The sounds of the little girl's laughter filled the sitting room as she stroked Mowgli's wet fur with a delicate hand on the hearthrug. Julia ushered Claire towards the fireplace, where a crackling fire behind a fireguard cast a warm glow over the toys scattered across the floor. She handed her a soft towel and a blanket, urging her to make herself comfortable.

As Claire towelled off, she took in the old-world charm of Julia's cottage. The space was small and cosy, filled with mismatched furniture and framed photographs on every surface. There were pictures of the little girl with dark curls over the past few years, pictures of Julia and Barker at the local church on their wedding day, ones of Jessie looking like a moodier teenager. There were pictures of Mowgli too, small and less fluffy but no less majestic.

"I can't believe he's back," Julia said as she settled on the sofa. "Where on earth did you find him?"

"Oakwood nursing home, of all places."

"The nursing home?" Julia shook her head. "That's miles away."

"The field leading away from the nursing home connects to the side of the farm behind your house. I just walked over it." She perched on an armchair, wondering how much she should tell Julia. She'd come this far—there was no point in keeping it from her. "I used to have this neighbour. Mrs Beaton. She's… not well. Used to live on her own near me, but she started acting off. Early stages of dementia, the doctors said. We helped her find a home and Oakwood had the best specialist care for her.

But before she moved, she had a habit of... taking in people's cats."

"Ah."

"She always had cats, mind you," Claire added. "Had this army of them following her every time she left the house, but in the end, she had more than we could count. And when we started looking at their collar tags, we realised they weren't all hers. How could they be? Took us weeks, but we ended up reuniting quite a lot of cats with missing posters we found online. She always took care of them the best she could, but I don't think she really knew what she was doing. Not really."

Julia sighed. "It sounds that way."

"She handed Mowgli over when I explained the situation," she said. "Maybe they both wandered off too far and found each other?"

"I'm just so glad he's home," she said, smiling as Mowgli stuck a leg in the air to lick at his belly. "Where are my manners? I haven't offered you a cup of tea."

"Coffee, if you have it."

"Coffee it is." Julia scooped up the little girl and said, "Come on, Olivia. Lunchtime for you."

After one last look at Mowgli, Julia disappeared into the kitchen, leaving Claire to soak in the fire's warmth. She couldn't help but feel a twinge of envy as she glanced around the cosy cottage.

This was the kind of life she'd been dreaming of

having with Ryan. A home to call their own. Her thoughts drifted to Mrs Beaton's old house back in Northash, and she hoped Sally was working on those miracles.

As she waited for Julia to return with the coffee, Claire wandered into the small bathroom and threw the damp towel into the washing basket. In the mirror, she ran a comb through her hair, flat to her head from the rain. Back in the hallway, she followed the sound of the boiling kettle passing by a slightly open door. She peeked through into the dining room, expecting to see the typical setup. Instead, there was an investigation board on the wall, not unlike the ones her father used to create at the station.

Jessie and a man Claire assumed to be Julia's husband, Barker, stood in front of the board, deep in discussion. They were so engrossed in their conversation that they didn't notice Claire's presence until Jessie caught her gaze. With a quick motion, Jessie shut the door, leaving Claire with more questions than answers. Julia left the kitchen, a steaming mug of coffee in hand. She handed it to Claire, a sheepish look on her face.

"I suppose you saw the board," she said. "The case has been on my mind constantly. The poisoned elderflower in my café, the murder right outside the church... I can't seem to ignore it."

Claire nodded, understanding Julia's preoccupation all too well.

"I feel the same way," she admitted, sipping the hot coffee. "It's hard not to get involved when it's happening right in front of you."

Julia motioned for Claire to follow her, and they walked into the dining room. The investigation board loomed large on one wall, covered in notes and photographs of all the suspects. Red string connected various pieces of evidence, forming a complex web of connections.

"Claire, this is my daughter, Jessie, and my husband, Barker," Julia said, gesturing to each of them. "Claire is here for the bowls tournament, and... she just brought Mowgli home. She found him."

Barker's face lit up at the news as he wrapped his arm around Julia's shoulder.

"Thank goodness," he said. Turning to Claire, he extended his hand. "Thank you so much for finding him. We've been worried sick."

Claire shook his hand, returning his smile.

"I'm glad I could help."

"We've met in the café, but good to meet you properly," Jessie said, shaking Claire's hand. "Where did you find him?"

"It's a long story," Julia said, her focus already shifting back to the investigation board. "And we have more present things to discuss." She turned to Claire, her expression serious. "You seem to have a nose for this sort of stuff," she said, gesturing to the board. "Maybe you could look over our notes and share anything we don't already know?"

Claire stepped closer to the board, her eyes scanning the various pieces of evidence. She recognised some names and faces—Gordon, Robert, Betty—but they weren't focusing on the other two men yet.

"I spoke with Malcolm and Henry earlier," Claire offered. "They mentioned Gordon and Robert used to be work friends, but things soured after Robert had an affair with Betty."

Julia nodded. "I heard about that in the café while it was happening."

"And apparently, Betty is in both Gordon's and Robert's wills. And earlier, at the nursing home, I overheard a heated exchange between Betty and Gordon. They were arguing about a secret Betty was apparently keeping for Gordon, and he... he accused her of being seen picking foxglove flowers."

"Weird timing to be a coincidence," Jessie muttered as Julia scribbled down the information at the table. "What did she say to that?"

"That he knew she liked the flowers, and they went in a vase. He accused her of being a 'scarlet woman' and she... she slapped him right across the face."

"Sounds pretty suspicious to me," Jessie said. "She must be behind all of this?"

Claire shrugged, not wanting to commit to accusing Betty just yet. Julia and Barker looked less sure, with Barker going as far as to shake his head.

"Let's not rush to conclusions," he cautioned. "We need to gather more evidence before pointing fingers."

"Barker is a former DI turned private investigator," Julia explained. "He's just being thorough."

"My father is a retired DI as well," Claire said. "DI Alan Harris. He worked in Northash."

"DI Harris?" Barker said, staring off into his memories. "Is he the guy who cracked the Northash Strangler case back in '98?"

"That rings a bell."

He laughed. "Small world. How is he these days?"

"Gardening a lot."

"That case made him something of a legend when I was coming up," he said, while Julia added the fresh notes to the wall. "They said he was like a dog with a bone when he was on a case."

"I think I inherited—"

The sound of the front door opening cut Claire off. Julia, Barker, and Jessie shared the same unsurprised—if not, irritated—looks as though they knew who to expect.

"*Julia?*" Dot's voice filled the hallway. "Have you heard the latest?"

"In here, Gran."

Dot burst in with two dogs at her side, both in red raincoats that matched Dot's. She flung down her hood, her eyes narrowing on Claire like they had in the bathroom at The Comfy Corner.

"I want a word with you!" Dot said, clutching both leads in one hand so she could point a condemning finger at Claire. "I just heard your *dreadful* grandmother in the café talking about *me*. Accusing *me*… she's telling anyone who'll listen that *I* killed Robert. That *I* poisoned Gordon."

"Haven't you been doing the same all week about her, Dot?" Jessie said with an amused smile. "People are probably taking her as seriously as they're taking you."

"I've only been saying that because I knew she's been saying it about me!" Dot insisted. "*This* is why I don't like tourists. They come in here, thinking they can run about the place getting involved in our local affairs… it's *ludicrous*."

"I'm glad some of them are getting involved," Julia said, standing by Claire's side. "This 'tourist' brought Mowgli home. She found him at the nursing home."

"Oh." Dot's scrunched expression softened as though she couldn't imagine such a thing. "Well… I… thank you. That's… wonderful news."

"I'll try to tell my gran to reel it in," Claire offered. "But I can't promise. She's a law unto herself."

"Sounds like someone I know," Julia said, half under her breath. Louder, she said, "How did you know Claire was here, anyway? This is a long way to come in the rain to have a go at a 'tourist.'"

"I'm not here for *that*," Dot said, her tight smile aimed at Claire verging on apologetic. "Claire's grandmother isn't the only one spreading gossip. There's a new rumour flying around the village about Betty."

"You're late," Jessie said. "Claire just told us about the will rumour."

"Not *that*. That's yesterday's news." Dot could hardly contain her smile. "Betty has been *arrested*!"

CHAPTER THIRTEEN

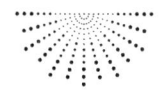

At the breakfast table in the B&B the next morning, Claire had her little black book open next to her plate. Rather than making notes for the café-inspired candle like she intended, the blue nib of the pen scribbled around in nonsensical spirals.

"You used to do that when we were in school," Ryan said from across the table, glancing up from that morning's copy of *The Peridale Post*. "Remember when Mrs Heys flipped out when you handed in your maths coursework covered in them?"

"Helps with concentration."

"Didn't you fail your maths coursework?" Greta said.

"Then it worked as well as it is now." She slapped the notepad shut, throwing the pen down by her half-finished breakfast. "I can't figure out what's going on with this case, so I thought I'd try to work on a scent formula. But I can't focus on that either." She nodded at the paper, the headline reading 'BASHED AT THE BOWLS.' "Anything new in there?"

"Not that you haven't already told me." He folded the paper in half, tucking it under his plate. "It's already outdated, anyway. Nothing about Betty's arrest in there."

"Well, the next issue will hopefully declare the case as *closed*," Greta said with a definite nod. "And now the gossiping can stop about us 'tourists' going on a murder spree. The *looks* people have been giving me..."

"The attention has been rather fabulous," Eugene countered. "If not a little persistent."

"What if Betty isn't behind this?" Claire suggested, the same thought that had kept her awake for most of the night after leaving Julia's cottage.

"The police wouldn't have arrested Betty if they didn't know for certain that she did it," Greta said, finishing her toast before reaching across Amelia to grab the newspaper from underneath Ryan's plate. "And you said it yourself, Claire. The foxgloves... the slap... this was all just a messy love triangle gone wrong and nothing to do with the tournament."

"It's like we're living through a teatime soap opera," Eugene said. "Scandals and slayings. It's all been rather exciting, but here's to today's tournament continuing without further interruption." He raised his orange juice in a toast. "Now this nasty murder business is behind us, we can focus on doing what we came to do—we'll take that trophy home."

"And I hope the Peridale team drops out."

"Who's being the bad sport now, Gran?" Claire said.

"Bad or not, it'll work in our favour," she said, unfolding the newspaper. "I hope you had a good night's sleep and are in top form. I have a good feeling about today. How's your wrist feeling, Eugene?"

"A little better," he said, flexing it slightly. "I was so sure it was broken. Almost feels silly that we waited for five hours in accident and emergency for the nurse to tell me it was a sprain and send me on my way with two paracetamol."

"A very *minor* sprain, at that," Greta pointed out. "Do you think you can play?"

"I should be able to throw left-handed if it starts hurting too much."

"We can't take the risk," Greta said, abandoning the paper before she'd read a word. She folded it and tapped on Amelia's head, then Hugo's, disrupting them from their slow cereal eating. "Hurry up and finish your breakfast. I'm going to teach you the rules, just in case. We need four players to qualify and there's no lower age limit."

"But I don't want to play bowls," Amelia whined, her face scrunching. "It's so *boring*."

Hugo nodded in agreement. "Yeah, it's like real bowling without the fun."

"Give it a go." Ryan chuckled, ruffling Hugo's hair. "I didn't think I'd enjoy it, but it's rather fun. Isn't it, Claire?"

"The most fun I've had all year."

"Liar," Amelia muttered, sliding off her chair.

Despite their groaning, they followed Greta and Eugene outside to practise.

"I'm going to sneak in a quick run around the village," Ryan said, kissing Claire on the cheek. "Won't be too long."

Claire finished her cold toast, the crunch echoing in the now-empty dining room. With a sigh, she pocketed her book, in no mood for candle making today. She settled into one of the armchairs by the front window, looking out on the vibrant garden outside. Before her mind ran away with itself raking over the confusing details of the case again, she decided to call the shop.

"*Claire's Candles*," came the warm, familiar voice of her father, though slightly masked by his posh phone voice. "Alan speaking. How can I help?"

"It's me, Dad," she said, a smile spreading across her face.

"Morning, little one," he said, and Claire felt a little more at ease. "We've been following the news. I hear there's been an arrest?"

"That's what the gossips have been saying." Claire shifted in the armchair, her phone pressed to her ear as she listened to the familiar buzz of her shop in the background. "How's everything going there?"

"Oh, you know, business as usual. Your mother's been keeping us all on our toes. Sales are good. Nothing to worry about."

As if on cue, Janet's voice rang out in the background, barking orders at Damon. Claire was sure she heard something about "lift with your back" and had terrible visions of her mother rearranging her entire shop. She looked out at the garden, taking a calming breath as she watched the pink foxgloves swaying in the breeze. The shop could wait till she got back.

"The poison used on Gordon... it was foxglove."

"Foxglove, eh? Like with Nigella, the beekeeper at the garden centre here last spring." He hummed to himself as he mulled over the information. "Well, it can't have been a strong dose if he walked away unscathed the day after. Nigella's heart gave out that same day, so I suppose he was lucky."

"Maybe whoever poisoned Gordon didn't understand the dosages?"

There was a pause on the other end of the line, and Claire could almost hear the gears turning in her father's mind. In the quiet, she was sure she heard the grating of wood against the shop floor as though something was being moved.

"Or maybe they understood how lethal it was and didn't intend to kill him at all?" he suggested after a moment.

"Why go to the trouble of poisoning someone if not to kill them?"

"To scare someone? A warning?" he said, his voice low and conspiratorial. "Think about it… if you're going to poison someone, you're more likely to over-fragrance the candle wax, so to speak. You'd want to make sure the poison did its job."

"Good point."

"Something to think about," he said. "But like you said, word on the street is the police made an arrest, so maybe they have their culprit?"

"Hopefully." Claire leaned back in the armchair, looking outside. Across the street, she saw Barker chatting with DI Moyes outside the station. "I met another retired DI yesterday."

"Oh?"

"Barker Brown?"

"Hmm. Not sure I've heard of him."

"Well, he's heard of you," she said, a hint of pride in her voice. "He remembered some 1998 case?"

"Ah, yes. That'll be the Northash Strangler," he said, a

touch of nostalgia in his tone. "My biggest case, up until that point. Rather tricky."

"Legendary, apparently."

"Funny what people remember about you, isn't it?" he said, gathering his thoughts for a moment—Claire sensed one of his old case stories on the way. "That one all came down to a messy love triangle. The police, the press, the public… they were dead set on stringing up the woman's husband. He barely showed any emotion after she was found strangled in Starfall Park, and people did what they do best."

"Filled in the blanks with wild accusations?"

"Exactly, but to me, the fella seemed like he was in shock. I saw him crying in his cell. The rest of the station said they were the tears of a guilty man, but I saw grief. I was the only one who thought he was innocent. We interviewed him over and over, to the point where most people would confess, but he never did. He just didn't strike me as a murderer."

"What did you do?"

"Against the advice of everyone who thought they knew better, I went against my fellow officers' judgments and found out the truth." He exhaled for a moment as though he were reliving the gritty details. "And I was right. She was strangled by her brother over an inheritance squabble. I knew I wasn't going to get a confession out of him, so I had to catch him in the act."

"How'd you do that?"

"I set a trap. I noticed marks on his girlfriend's neck, like she'd been choked." He sighed, his voice almost a whisper. "The poor girl wouldn't tell me anything, but I could see the truth in her eyes. She was terrified around him, so I... I pretended to be her."

"Did you get into drag, Dad?"

"Not on *that* occasion," he said, chuckling. "I studied her handwriting the best I could and wrote the brother a little letter, telling him I knew what he'd done. I kept it vague. Let him fill in the blanks, and he did. I convinced his girlfriend to go out that evening, and I waited at her house. In her bed, to be exact. Pretended to be sleeping. And then... then he came in and tried to strangle me."

"Crikey."

"Thankfully, I had a few officers who agreed to go along with the out-of-the-box plan waiting in the wardrobe." He let out a sigh of relief. "They said I was crazy... unprofessional... unorthodox... but I was proud of that case. I stopped an innocent man being charged, and I don't think we would have got the truth any other way."

"You're a hero, Dad."

"I was just doing my job, little one," he said, his tone brightening up again. "So, this arrest... given that you've called me and you're not celebrating, I'm going to assume you think the local plod have arrested the wrong person?"

"She *could* have done it," Claire said, glancing outside at Barker, still talking with Moyes—they were deep in conversation about something serious. "Betty has motive, means, and she was in the right place at the right time for both incidents."

"But?"

"A niggling feeling."

"The old niggling feeling. I say you listen to it, Claire and—Oh, I'm going to pass you over. Someone wants to talk to you."

"Hey, Claire," Damon said a second later. "So, I hear you're tangled up in another murder? Even on holiday, you can't help yourself."

"Enough about that. Are you helping my mother rearrange the shop?"

"...*no*."

"Damon..."

"The shop is just as you left it," he said, even less convincingly. "Say what you want about your mother, but she is a tough negotiator. She's been upselling *everyone* on *everything*. I don't think the shop has ever made so much profit in a week."

"Maybe I should just stay in Peridale? Sounds like you don't need me."

"Please don't leave me here with her," he whispered.

There was a pause, and then Damon, still whispering, said, "Has Sally called you yet?"

"No," she said, her stomach knotting at the whisper. "Why?"

"She's probably waiting till her break."

"Is it about…" she couldn't bring herself to say 'the mortgage.'

"She'll call you."

The knot tightened.

"You should get back to work," she said, forcing lightness into her voice. "Outsell the up-seller. Or I'll replace you with my mother."

"But then you'd have to work with her every day," he teased.

"Fair point."

They hung up, and Claire turned to Evelyn, who was dusting a shelf filled with an eclectic array of trinkets and crystals.

"I couldn't help but overhear you talking about the arrest," Evelyn started, dusting closer to Claire. "When I was meditating in the garden early this morning, I saw the police release Betty from the station across the road. Unless I was seeing things, she's already a free woman."

"Released?" The knot in Claire's stomach loosened as she jumped out of the armchair. "Betty said she lived in a place called Wellington Heights. Have you heard of it?"

Evelyn's hand stilled, the feather duster hovering over a wooden box with intricate carvings.

"You're not thinking of visiting, are you?" Evelyn said, drawing Claire in close. "That place… that place has a *dark* aura."

CHAPTER FOURTEEN

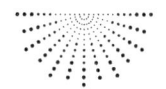

Wellington Heights came into view on the horizon at the top of a winding private driveway. The huge sandstone manor reminded Claire of the house in Starfall Park back home, its imposing presence both familiar and unsettling.

In her fist, she clenched a small purple chunk of amethyst, a crystal Evelyn had thrust upon her before she left the B&B. The smooth, cool surface pressed against her palm while Evelyn's grumblings about the place being 'cursed' echoed around in her mind.

The sound of a car horn startled Claire from her thoughts. She moved to step out of the way, turning to see Julia's vintage wheels pulling up alongside her.

"It's a long driveway," Julia called as she rolled down the window. "Fancy a lift?"

Claire climbed in, the old car creaking beneath her as she settled in.

"So," Julia started, "we must have both heard that Betty was released this morning."

"Evelyn saw her leaving the station."

"My gran saw it too, with her binoculars from her window," Julia said with a disapproving sigh. "She likes to keep an eye on the village when things go awry. And when nothing is going awry."

"Sounds like she needs a hobby."

"She cycled through them all, and this is the one she settled on. A touch of neighbourhood watch with a side of the occasional vigilante justice."

"Peridale's very own Batman." They both laughed. "Has she given away any more about her alibi?"

Julia shook her head, her gaze drifting to the crystal in Claire's palm.

"From Evelyn," Claire explained.

"I have a whole drawer of them," she said with an amused smile. "She hands them out like sweets."

"Apparently, I needed protection to come here. She said Wellington Heights was cursed."

As they approached the old manor, its shadow ominously swallowing up the sunlight, Julia's expression turned pensive. "I don't believe in curses, but Wellington Heights has certainly had its fair share of bad luck." They pulled into the car park, Julia's old car standing out among the sleek, modern vehicles. She stared up at the imposing building and continued, "The manor used to belong to my stepmother, Katie Wellington, before she sold it to a developer, James Jacobson."

"Name rings a bell. I think he tried to buy Starfall House back home."

"Tried?"

"I know the owner and she didn't want it converted into flats."

"Then you got a lucky escape," Julia whispered. "He just tried to tear down half of our village to build his fantasy development. For all their faults, the people of Peridale came together to put a stop to his schemes. Haven't seen him around for a while." She pulled the keys from the ignition. "Before all of that, he turned this place into apartments, but that was probably for the best. Back when this was Wellington Manor, let's just say it earned its cursed reputation. Secrets, bankruptcy, murder… and the rest."

"Let's hope the curse takes a day off today," Claire said, pocketing the stone. "So, how are we doing this?"

"Let's be honest with her," Julia said, climbing out. "Hopefully it inspires the same from her. I'd quite like to know what inspired her to slap Gordon yesterday."

"You and me both."

They approached the grand doors of the building, and after scanning the intercom system, Claire jammed the

'B. Fletcher' button while Julia reached into her handbag to retrieve a white cardboard box.

"Betty... it's Julia... from the café," she called, her voice friendly yet firm. "I brought you some cakes."

"I... I didn't order any cakes." Betty sounded tired.

"Can we come in?" Julia said.

"We?"

"It's Claire, Betty," Claire said, leaning forward, mirroring Julia's friendly tone. "From the Northash team?"

"What is it with you two..."

Betty's sigh crackled through the speaker, followed by a moment of silence.

"What kind of cake?"

"Battenberg. Your favourite, isn't it?"

The door buzzed, signalling that it had been unlocked. Claire and Julia exchanged a pleased glance before stepping inside.

"Works every time," Julia said, patting the cake box.

"Would work on me."

Inside, Claire marvelled at the grand entrance hall of Wellington Heights. A crystal chandelier hung overhead, casting a dazzling array of light across the polished marble floor. A sweeping staircase curved gracefully, leading to the upper floors of the converted manor. In the air, Claire picked up on a sweet fragrance like bergamot, though she couldn't see any candles or diffusers.

One of the doors on the ground floor swung open, revealing Betty, who squinted at them with tired, annoyed eyes.

"What is this? *Cagney and Lacey?*" she muttered, swinging the door wider. "Make this quick. I'm not feeling too good. The police barely let me get a wink of sleep last night." She took the cake box from Julia. "How about I make some tea to go along with this?"

They both accepted the offer, but as they followed Betty into the luxurious apartment, Claire noticed a bunch of foxglove flowers poking out of the bin. She nodded towards them, catching Julia's eye. Julia acknowledged the discovery with a subtle nod of her own.

They settled around a marble kitchen island, the smooth surface gleaming under the soft light. Julia looked around, taking in the elegant surroundings.

"This place is nice," she commented, her fingers tracing the cool marble. "This whole apartment used to be the kitchen."

"Must have been a big kitchen," Claire thought aloud.

"That was the Wellingtons for you," Julia said.

Betty brought over two steaming cups of tea to the island, setting them down with a weary sigh. She climbed onto a stool as though the movement pained her.

"I was never supposed to end up here," Betty admitted, taking in the elegant apartment. "I bought it with my half of the divorce settlement." She took a sip of her tea, a faraway look in her eyes. "Gordon's plan was always that we'd get to seventy-five, sell our house, and move into Oakwood. We'd live our lives being waited on hand and foot between playing tennis and watching television." A bitter laugh escaped her lips. "Life didn't work out that way. He went ahead with his plan by himself, but especially after the divorce, I wasn't ready to feel that old. After I ended things with Gordon, I realised I had some independence left in the tank."

Claire glanced at her tea. Betty was sipping hers, but Julia hadn't reached for hers either.

"I heard it was the other way around," Claire said. "That he left you because you were having a years-long affair with Robert?"

"Yes, that's the gossip around the village." She shook her head, slicing off some of the Battenberg with her gold-plated fork. "They're also saying I *wormed* my way into both of their wills. I admit I was once in Gordon's will, given that we *were* married for thirty years. But I don't know *or* care if that's still the case. I imagine it's not. And yes, I was in Robert's will, but I certainly didn't *worm* my way in." The cake went into her mouth, but she had more to add. "And we were *not* having an affair. Not in the way Gordon and the rest of them say, anyway."

"In what way, then?" Julia asked. "You must have been close if Robert would put you in his will?"

Betty reached across the counter and pulled forward an ornate jewellery box, unclasping it with a gentle click. She showed them a pile of glittering gemstones set among tangles of gold chains and rings.

"I was a nurse," she continued, snapping the lid shut. "As I started to slow down in life, so did my work. The wards were gruelling. You'll know all about that with your sister, Julia."

Julia nodded. "Sue has told me some horror stories."

"Unlike Sue, I stuck around for years longer than I should have. I wore myself out, and then I had enough. I became a private sector carer for the elderly, and I looked after Robert's mother, Prudence, in her final days. Prudence wanted me to have her jewellery collection when she died." She laughed at the memory, running her fingers across the details on the lid of the box. "Silly really. She'd put all her jewellery on every day to sit at home watching *Bargain Hunt* and *Songs of Praise* like she was out at the opera. And I would always comment on how pretty she looked. It was only polite. She went to all that effort every day, after all." She looked down at her own hands, bare aside from a wedding ring. "I was never one for excessive jewellery." She rolled the ring around a few times before clenching her fist. "Prudence didn't have any female relatives, so she promised she'd leave me the jewellery in her will."

"That was nice of her," Julia said.

"I always told her she didn't have to," Betty said defensively. "Like I said, I was mostly being polite to cheer her up, and she died before she ever got around to changing it. The jewellery went to Robert, and to honour his mother's wishes, he said he'd give it to me. I said I was in no rush to get it, so he put it in his will. That's all." Her eyes met Claire's and then moved to Julia, a fierce determination burning within them. "I did *not* kill Robert for a box of tacky jewellery. I don't need the money. The hospital might not have paid well, but Prudence was wealthy and generous with my salary. Years of caring for her, along with the divorce settlement, saw that I'd be well taken care of in my final years."

"So, if it wasn't an affair with Robert," Claire said, gentle but probing, "what was it? You looked rather close in the café... talking about how you both wanted Gordon off the team."

Betty took a long, deep slurp of her tea. Claire and Julia still hadn't touched theirs.

"I won't deny... deny..." She paused, a coughing fit interrupting her words. When it subsided, she continued, her voice strained. "Gordon was intent on ruining the team with his micromanaging ways. He was always the same, even in our marriage. Everything had to be *his* way.

Never took anyone else's thoughts or feelings on board." She pursed her lips, picking up the cup with both hands. "You know he used to drink? *A lot*. I used to beg him to stop, and it never made any difference. He only stopped when he almost lost his job, and he *still* wonders why they promoted Robert over him."

"And your relationship with Robert?" Julia pushed, seemingly picking up on the fact she'd dodged Claire's question. "I hate to quote the gossips, but they've had a lot to say about the two of you over the last few months."

"We *were* close," she admitted with an almost defeated sigh. "I was at his mother's house almost every day for years, and he was a good son. He visited often. I'd always known him through Gordon, but we developed a bond of our own. He became an emotional support for me. He listened to me in a way that Gordon never had." A single tear escaped, rolling down Betty's cheek. She batted it away, her voice trembling. "It's true. I loved Robert, but it never went further than holding hands. Not so much as a kiss."

As Betty cried, Julia reached out, her hand resting on Betty's arm in a comforting gesture. She plucked a handkerchief from her bag with the other.

"I understand," Julia said. "My first husband was like that. I don't think I realised how bad until I met my second husband."

Claire sat back, thinking of Ryan and his gentle,

tender ways. She'd been single for most of her adult life, with nothing to compare to Ryan.

"It was at Prudence's funeral, just before Christmas," Betty began, twisting the handkerchief around her fingers. "Gordon saw us holding hands. It was during Prudence's wake. I was inconsolable. I didn't want to lose my routine, and I was facing the idea of *his* plan to move to the nursing home. But that's what Gordon wanted. His plan, controlled to the last detail."

"That's when Gordon says he ended things," Julia said.

Betty shook her head. "Gordon blew up at me, but he didn't want to end the marriage. *I* ended the marriage when Gordon retaliated by having an *actual* affair with Emily."

"Ah," Claire said.

"Emily was in nursing too before she became a paramedic," Betty explained, her voice tinged with pain. "She was my friend once. My neighbour, too. I never thought I'd end my marriage after so many years, but I decided I was ready for a clean break." A regretful sigh escaped Betty's lips. "I wish I'd moved things further with Robert, but we were both so paralysed by everyone watching us. The rumours spread, the rumours *keep* spreading, so much so even the police took them seriously."

Another coughing fit seized Betty, and she reached for her tea, taking a sip to soothe her throat. Claire's phone rang in her pocket, and she was about to ignore it when she saw it was from Sally. Excusing herself, Claire walked to the back of the apartment, stopping by a set of double doors that overlooked the lawn at the back. A young couple played with two children, all laughing without a care in the world.

As soon as Claire answered, Sally's voice confirmed her fears from Damon's hint earlier.

"Not good news, mate," Sally said bleakly. "I know I said I could work miracles, but I can't seem to make these numbers work."

"Ah."

"You either need a bigger deposit, or you need to drive the price down by fifty grand, but it's already forty under value."

Claire watched as the young family rushed back into their house, the first drops of rain beginning to fall.

"It's okay," she said, trying to mask her disappointment with a smile. "It was too good to be true, anyway."

"Mate?" Sally sighed. "I... I'm sorry. I know you had your heart set on that cul-de-sac, but there are other houses. When you get back—"

"We'll figure something out. Thanks for trying, Sal, I—"

The sound of a cup shattering made Claire spin

around. She turned back to see Julia catching Betty as she slumped on her stool against the island.

"I'll call you back."

Claire hung up and rushed back into the kitchen as Julia struggled to support the older woman's weight. Betty's face contorted in pain, her hand clutching at her chest as she gasped for air.

"What's happening?"

"She... she said she felt like she had heartburn and then she started convulsing. I... I don't know."

"Is she having a heart attack?"

Betty groaned, her eyes fluttering open as she looked up at Claire and Julia. Her lips parted as if to speak, but no words came out. Instead, she wilted onto the cold marble.

"*Betty?*" Claire called. "Betty, can you hear me?"

Claire pressed her fingers against Betty's neck, searching for a pulse. She held her breath, hoping, praying for a sign of life. But there was nothing.

Betty was gone.

And there they were.

The foxgloves poking out of the bin.

"We must not be the first visitors Betty had that morning."

CHAPTER FIFTEEN

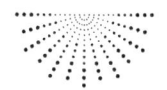

Back at the village green, the teams had once again gathered for the continuation of the tournament. From the looks of it, the first match was underway—Northash versus Chipping Norton, with the Northash team having recruited two new members. Despite their complaints at breakfast about the game being too dull, Amelia and Hugo were now fully engaged. News of the death at Wellington Heights had not yet reached the village, and the remnants of the Peridale team were nowhere to be seen.

"*Where* have you been?" Greta demanded upon noticing Claire. "I know you don't care about this tournament as much as I do, but it's not fair for you to just disappear like—"

"Betty's dead, Gran."

"W-what? In prison?"

"She was released due to a lack of evidence. I visited her with Julia to ask some questions. One minute we were talking, and the next—" Claire clenched her eyes shut at the image of Betty's colour draining away, her face pressed against the chilling white marble. "It looked like she might have had a heart attack."

"Oh, dear. That poor woman. Do you think the stress caused it?"

"Perhaps, but given everything that's been going on lately, it would be a gigantic coincidence if Betty wasn't murdered."

"*Murder?*" echoed around them, the whispers carrying on the wind, and Claire watched the jovial spirit drain from the air as word spread around the green. The game ground to a halt, the bowls abandoned.

"Look at her." Greta's eyes cut across the green to the café, where Dot was observing the proceedings from behind the window. "I haven't seen her *all* morning, and *now* she's shown her face after another member of her team has turned up dead?"

"Don't make a scene, Gran," Claire cautioned. "I don't think Dot..."

But Greta was already marching towards the café, her face set in a determined scowl. Eugene hurried behind, keen not to miss the action. Ryan hung back with the kids, but Claire knew someone needed to play referee and caught up before Greta reached the window.

"Get out here," Greta demanded, planting her hands on her hips. "Face your public, Dorothy South. You can't hide this time."

"I *beg* your pardon?"

"You heard me," Greta pressed. "You're always lurking about, turning up in the right place at the wrong time. You've been missing all morning, but here you are, as if butter wouldn't melt, and Betty's body isn't even cold on the slab."

"Betty's... *body?*"

"Don't play coy with me."

However, to Claire, Dot's bewilderment at the news seemed genuine.

"I can assure you, this is the first I've heard—"

"Likely story," Greta cried, pushing open the front door. "Come on. Show yourself. Let's settle this like real women."

"Are you trying to... *fight* me?"

"If it's a fight you want, it's a fight you'll get." Greta rolled her sleeves up in a flash, and Claire wedged herself between Greta and the café door. "I know you've been telling people that I'm behind all this mischief."

"I most certainly do *not* want to fight," Dot protested, looking down her nose at Greta from the café. "I don't know how you do things up north, but we're a little more civilised down here."

"*Civilised*? We're practically tripping over bodies out here, and I'd wager it's all your doing."

"You feral *beast*!"

"Who are you calling a beast?"

"Enough," Claire demanded, fixing them both with a stern look. "A woman has just died—probably murdered—and you two are bickering like children. Show some respect."

Dot and Greta fell silent, their eyes downcast.

"Yes, well…" Greta cleared her throat. "Perhaps I got a bit carried away, but I just want to understand what's happening around here."

"And I *don't*?" Dot replied, her lips pursed, though her tone softened. "I apologise for calling you a beast."

"And I apologise for not being more civilised," Greta responded. Claire nudged her with her elbow, prompting her to add, "And for making you think I was about to fight you. I wouldn't have touched a perfectly curled grey hair on your head."

"Hmm."

"Hmm."

"How about a hug?" Eugene suggested. "To clear the air?"

"Absolutely not," Dot declared, turning on her heels

before disappearing through the beaded curtain at the back of the café.

"A *hug*, Eugene?" Greta shuddered at the thought. "I don't know if whatever stick she has up her backside is contagious."

"Gran…"

"Well, Claire, you heard her. All that stuff about us being from up north. She's looking down her nose at us from her ivory Cotswold castle, and I don't like it."

"You're giving her good reason to," Claire retorted.

"She might be right, dear," Eugene suggested, wrapping an arm around Greta's shoulders. "There is something about Dot that seems to bring out the worst in you, but knowing both of you, I'd say you might be cut from different ends of the same cloth."

"Watch it, Eugene," Greta warned, "or you might be the next one to have your head bashed in with a bowl."

Eugene led Greta back to the green, leaving Claire to step into the café. Dot busied making herself a pot of tea behind the counter, and beyond her, a misty haze of smoke seeped in from the kitchen. While Dot was distracted, scrambling under the counter for a tray, Claire slipped through the beads. Julia and Moyes were both seated on the back doorstep, looking across the small yard and through a gate that overlooked a sprawling field.

"Hope you don't mind if I interrupt?"

"Not at all," Julia said, shuffling over to make room for Claire between them. "DI Moyes was just asking for my theories, but a fresh perspective wouldn't hurt."

"Any perspective wouldn't hurt right now," Moyes admitted, pocketing her device. "I couldn't gather enough evidence to charge my prime suspect, and now she's dead. Paramedics at the scene said it looked like she might have died from a heart attack, just as you both mentioned, and it's only a matter of time before that toxicology report comes back looking like Gordon's."

"Only this time with much higher levels," Claire added, recalling her father's comments about the negligible amount of poison in Gordon's elderflower cordial. "Either the person behind all this didn't want to make the same mistake twice, or they never intended to kill Gordon in the first place."

"You mean to say you think Gordon was poisoned as some sort of warning?"

"It's just an idea." Claire sighed as she gazed at the field stretching endlessly into the distance. "I'm as stumped as you, Detective. I was starting to suspect Betty after the rumours, but after talking to her, I believed her."

"I felt the same," Julia agreed. "The way she opened up felt so raw. I'd already discounted her before she…" She exhaled, dropping her head. "I wish there was something I could have done. Those foxgloves in the bin should have rung alarm bells."

"Betty said she liked to put them in a vase," Claire reminded her. "Perhaps she couldn't bear to look at them after the police released her. And she's not the only one with a direct link to foxgloves."

"Malcolm's garden?" Moyes asked.

Claire nodded. "I visited him yesterday, on Betty's suggestion. She pointed the finger at him, and he pointed it back at her. And now one of them is dead, and…"

Her voice trailed off as her thoughts wandered back to her visit to Malcolm's vibrant garden, particularly her hasty exit, before the search for Mowgli pulled her away.

"I tripped over something yesterday in Malcolm's garden," Claire recalled. "It was poking out of the flower bed, right on the edge. It was smooth, round, and had some weight to it…"

"Like a bowling ball?" Julia suggested.

"I'm not sure," Claire admitted. "I was going to check, but then I got a call from the nursing home. It slipped my mind until now. It could have been just an ordinary stone, but there was something about the way it felt against my shoe that made me curious."

"Then let's hope it's still there," Moyes said, rising to her feet. "From now on, I think it's best if you both keep your distance from this case. I got the impression that Betty was withholding something during her interviews last night, and given the timing of her death, I'm assuming she knew something crucial. If you stumble upon the same thing... I don't want another pair of bodies on my hands." She unclipped her radio and started towards the courtyard. "Puglisi, I need a search team at Malcolm's..."

DI Moyes hurried off to investigate the potential clue at Malcolm's garden, the detective's parting words resonating in Claire's mind. It would be easy to surrender and return home. She could be back in Northash by dinner time if she left within the hour. Back home, in her shop, with her cats, confronting the reality of Sally's bad news. Given the circumstances that followed the ill-timed phone call, she hadn't dwelt much on the mortgage rejection—she still needed to tell Ryan, but that would have to wait.

"If Betty was killed for knowing too much," Claire began, "someone must be desperate to keep the truth hidden. Moyes is right... we might be in danger."

"Are you thinking of giving up?"

"I... I'm not sure. You?"

Julia met her gaze, a determined glint in her eyes.

"I don't think I could even if I wanted to," she admitted. "To kill Betty so soon after her arrest... whoever is behind this is getting sloppy. It's only a matter of time before they slip up."

"And speaking of tripping up," Claire said, massaging her temples. "That thing I tripped over in Malcolm's garden... if that was a half-buried bowling bowl..."

"The murder weapon that killed Robert, you mean?"

"If it was *that* bowl," Claire exhaled, "why would Malcolm want to kill all three of them? Given the land dispute with Gordon, I can see that one, and Betty accusing him… maybe she did know something about him?"

"He has the poison flowers in his garden."

"He does. But why kill Robert?"

"There's clearly something we're missing," Julia said, rising from the step. "But one thing is obvious to me—there's more that connects the three victims than just the bowls team."

"The love triangle," Claire confirmed.

"From where I'm standing, and given what Betty revealed, it's a love *square*," Julia remarked, pausing to look out at the field. "Have you spoken with the paramedic yet?"

"No. I saw her at the nursing home visiting Gordon once, but that's all. Have you?"

"Not yet." Julia turned back to Claire, her smile widening. "But I might have a way to get to Emily." She extended a hand to help Claire up. "If you're still in, that is?"

Claire grasped Julia's hand and replied, "Two heads are better than one. We've come too far to turn back now."

After leaving Julia to manage the growing queue of

customers that Dot had been struggling to serve in the café, Claire caught up with Ryan on his way back to the B&B with the children. She reached out, intertwining her fingers with his.

"There's something I need to tell you," she said, leaning her head on his shoulder. "It's about the mortgage, and I'm sorry, but… it's not good news."

CHAPTER SIXTEEN

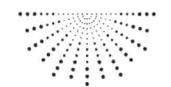

*C*laire groaned as she was shaken awake, her mind still groggy with sleep. For a moment, she thought it was one of her cats, Sid or Domino, demanding their breakfast, but the unfamiliar texture of the bed sheets reminded her that she was far from home. Opening her eyes, she found Granny Greta staring down at her.

"*Claire...* are you awake?"

"Not anymore," Claire grumbled, half-sitting up and surveying the room. Despite the bright sunlight peeking around the edges of the curtains, it felt like the middle of the night. She glanced at the empty space beside her and then across the room to the empty beds in the corner.

"You slept through your alarm," Greta explained, rummaging through Claire's bag. "Ryan didn't bother to wake you with all the running around you've been doing lately. He thought you'd appreciate the lie-in, but we're missing the action!"

"Action?" Claire's heart skipped a beat as Greta threw a t-shirt at her. "Has someone else been attacked?"

"Not yet," Greta replied, lifting Claire's arm to spray deodorant underneath it before cramming the t-shirt over her head backwards. "I was just in the front garden having a spot of tea with Eugene when we saw Dot and Henry sprinting through the village."

"Sprinting?"

"Fast walking," she corrected, flinging back the covers. "From what I could pick up, it sounds like Gordon has lost his mind and is destroying Malcolm's cottage."

Claire stumbled into a pair of jeans, her mind racing with questions as Greta's words echoed in her ears.

"They arrested Malcolm during the night," Greta said. "Evelyn said she was 'moon-bathing'—whatever that means—when she saw him being taken into the station. And then Eugene overheard at the café first thing this morning that they found the bowling bowl used to kill Robert."

"Seems I've slept through an eventful morning."

"And it's not over. Come on, let's get a wiggle on."

In her haste to drag Claire to the door, Greta knocked over the scent sample Claire had crafted the night before to distract herself. The loosely corked bottle toppled, spilling its contents across the bedroom floor. An aroma reminiscent of Julia's café filled the room, but not quite right.

"The Harris clumsiness strikes again," Greta exclaimed. "Claire, I'm sorry, I—"

"It was only a first test, and it wasn't right."

She grabbed her jacket and followed Greta out of the bedroom, her mind already shifting gears to the unfolding drama in the village. Greta moved with a giddy spring in her step, thrilled by the prospect of witnessing the latest development in the ongoing mystery.

"You're up!" Eugene cried, hopping from one foot to the other on the porch. "If we put some pep in our step, we might catch them up before they get to Malcolm's cottage."

"Lead the way!" Greta cried, charging ahead to the gate. "Which way to Malcolm's cottage?"

"Well, they went *that* way," Eugene said, pointing up the road. "Shouldn't be too difficult to find, should it?"

"It's this way," Claire said, taking the lead. "I've already been there twice."

Claire raced through the village, her heart pounding in her chest as she led Greta and Eugene down Mulberry Lane. They passed an antique shop, its windows filled with dusty trinkets and forgotten treasures, before turning onto an overgrown path near the allotments.

As they followed the winding path, the village fell

away behind them, replaced by a sea of green fields stretching out to the horizon. Finally, they reached Malcolm's cottage, nestled in the middle of nowhere. But instead of the inviting garden Claire remembered, they were greeted by a scene of chaos and destruction.

Gordon stood in the midst of it all, wielding a motorised hedge trimmer like a man possessed. The once-beautiful flowers lay in scattered heaps, their petals strewn across the ground.

Henry and Dot stood at the edge of the garden, their voices raised in protest. Henry, usually so mild-mannered, was red-faced and shouting at Gordon to stop. But Gordon seemed beyond reason.

"*This* is why he attacked me!" Gordon cried, his voice cracking with emotion. "Why he killed Robert... why he killed my Betty..."

Claire noticed a laser perimeter set up around the plot, marking the boundary of Gordon's smooth patch neighbouring Malcom's garden.

"Malcolm's garden border stops a metre *that* way," he declared. "I'm well within my rights to clear away what shouldn't be there."

As Gordon continued his rampage, mowing down row after row of flowers, Claire felt a pang of sympathy for Malcolm. She knew how much his garden meant to him, how much care and love he poured into every bloom. To see it destroyed like this was heart-breaking.

"Malcolm didn't kill anyone!" Henry cried, his voice rising above the chaos. "He wouldn't. It's not in his nature. He keeps himself to himself for a reason."

Gordon spun around, pointing the hedge trimmer in their direction.

"So why did the police arrest him?" he yelled, his face contorted with rage. "Why did he have the murder weapon in his garden?"

"It's *obvious* someone framed Malcolm," Dot cried. "He's not a stupid man. He wouldn't just leave a murder weapon half-buried in his garden for anyone to find it. *Nobody* would!"

But Gordon wasn't listening. He continued his assault on the garden, the hedge trimmer buzzing and whirring as it tore through the delicate flowers.

"I can't watch this anymore," Greta said, shaking her head. "If someone did this to my Alan's garden, it'd break his heart."

Without warning, Greta charged forward, crossing the laser lines. An alarm wailed in protest, but Greta paid it no heed. She marched straight up to Gordon and yanked the battery out of the back of the hedge trimmer.

The machine sputtered and died, and Gordon whirled around, his eyes blazing with fury. For a moment, it looked like he might attack Greta, but Eugene, Claire, and even Dot joined the fray, forming a human shield between them.

"Go on," Dot said, her voice ringing out across the garden. "Call the police. Have us all arrested for trespassing. Something tells me they have more important things to deal with right now."

"You're *out*," Gordon cried. "Both of you. You're off the team."

"We're not part of *your* team anymore," Dot declared. "You're on your own now, Gordon, and you need at least four people to enter the tournament."

"From where I'm standing, you're two short."

"Malcolm *will* be released," Dot said with a roguish smile, "and I've already found plenty of new members, enough to make up multiple teams to increase our chances of a Peridale win without you."

"You're lying," Gordon spat.

"We'll see about that when the tournament restarts, shall we? Good luck finding new members to control, Gordon. We're divorcing you."

With a final glare, Gordon stormed off towards his car, the engine roaring as he sped away. He narrowly missed Henry, who had to jump out of the way to avoid being hit.

"I wish that poison had worked," Henry muttered.

Dot turned to Greta, brushing a shredded petal off her shoulder.

"Are you hurt?"

Greta nodded. "I'm fine. He's not as scary as he likes

to think."

"No, he's not."

As they stood there, the pressure that had been simmering between them seemed to melt away, replaced by a newfound understanding.

"We can't leave it like this for Malcolm to come home to," Claire said as she took in the ruined garden. "It'll devastate him."

"You're right," Dot said, scratching at the back of her curls as she rolled the heads of ruined roses under her shoe. "We can't bring his garden back, but perhaps we could tidy things up a bit."

"Good idea," Greta agreed. "If only my Alan was here. He'd know what to do."

"I have the keys to one of the allotments just down the lane," Dot continued, patting her pocket. "We'll borrow some wheelbarrows and tools and get started putting things straight, and then I'll treat you all to lunch at the café. Call it a peace offering."

"Oh, that's very kind," Greta said, looping arms with Dot as they set off. "You know, I love that brooch you always wear. Is it an antique?"

Peace may have been reached between Dot and Greta, but there was no such peace in the air in Peridale. Glancing over her shoulder at the ruined garden, Claire couldn't help but feel responsible for the destruction.

If she hadn't tipped Moyes off about the bowl, the

garden might have remained intact and Malcolm a free man. If he hadn't been framed, why would Malcolm bury a murder weapon in such an obvious place?

CLAIRE WIPED THE SWEAT FROM HER BROW WITH THE BACK of her gloved hand, leaving a smudge of dirt across her forehead. They'd been working tirelessly all morning to clear away the destruction Gordon had left in his wake at Malcolm's garden. Dot, Eugene, Greta, and Henry had been working as one big—mostly happy—team scooping up the ruined flowers and piling them into wheelbarrows.

As the sun climbed higher in the sky, Percy arrived with a thermos of tea, offering a welcome break from their labouring. They gathered around, finding spots to sit amongst the debris. All except for Henry. He sat alone on Malcolm's doorstep, giving Claire the perfect opportunity to talk to him. He hadn't said a word since his strange poisoning comment earlier.

"Turning into quite a warm day," Claire said, trying to ease into the conversation as she perched on the upturned plant pot. "You must be used to working outside come rain or shine."

"I suppose I am."

"Been a postman for long?"

"I've been delivering mail in Peridale for decades," he stated. "I know every nook and cranny of this village." His expression shifted, becoming more guarded. "But that's not what you want to talk about, is it?"

"You got me," she said, offering him a tight smile. "I can't imagine how difficult it must have been for you to watch Malcolm's garden being destroyed like that. It's clear you care deeply about your friend."

"I've known Malcolm for years," he said, sighing. "He's a gentle soul. He wouldn't hurt a fly. Seeing it like this, it breaks my heart. I wish I'd had the courage to stand up to Gordon."

"He seems like a real piece of work."

"Gordon's the worst thing to happen to the team." His lips twisted into a sour snarl. "I've been on the team for twenty years, but Gordon has been on for five minutes in comparison. He installed himself as leader and made it his sole focus after retiring. A horrible, controlling man. I'd go as far as to call him a bully. I'm not surprised Betty looked elsewhere."

"Betty had a different view of her relationship with Robert. She said it was platonic."

"That's only because she cared too much about keeping up appearances. The fact is, she was in love with Robert. Everyone could see it, except for Gordon. He thought he had Betty exactly where he wanted her: his stay-at-home wife who'd cook his meals and iron his shirts while getting nothing in return. He kept her in a cage like a bird."

"Sounds old-fashioned."

"Now, I usually like old-fashioned, but certain attitudes should stay in the past for a reason," he said, staring down into the tea clutched in his hands. "But that's Gordon for you. Stuck in the past when it came to his marriage, but obsessed with the future when it came to the bowls team. He ruined the spirit of the game. There should never have been so much division on a simple bowls team. He needed teaching a lesson."

"I suppose he got one," Claire said, the killer question on the tip of her tongue. "I heard you this morning. You said you wished the poison had worked on Gordon."

"It was just a... thoughtless remark," he said, staring around the shredded garden. "I was upset... I didn't mean anything by it. Not really. But I..." Sighing, he looked at Claire properly for the first time since she sat down. "I did notice the foxglove in Malcolm's garden, and after reading that article, I'd be lying if I said the thought hadn't crossed my mind."

"What article?"

"There was an article in *Cotswold Gardening Magazine* about a beekeeper who was poisoned with foxglove up north."

Claire's heart skipped a beat. She knew exactly which beekeeper Henry was referring to, but she chose not to reveal her personal connection. Instead, she focused on the implications of Henry's words.

"That's a pretty damning thing to admit, Henry."

"I know," he said, his voice filled with regret. "But I only *thought* about it. That's it. A cruel, morbid thought passing by. I never acted on it. I would never."

"Did Malcolm read the article too?"

"Most people did," Henry replied. "It's a popular magazine, and I delivered one to almost every house in the village."

"You must get around the village quite a lot on your mail route," she said. "Have you noticed anything unusual lately?"

"I dropped off some post at the nursing home yesterday morning, and I saw Betty coming out," he confided. "I'm unsure of the exact time, but it was a good few hours before she was found dead."

"I saw Betty visiting Gordon there myself a few days ago."

"I know that's not entirely unusual on the surface. Old habits die hard, and they were intent on keeping things civil for the sake of appearances. But under the surface…" He half-rolled his eyes. "They *resented* each other. She could barely look at him most days."

"I got that impression."

"For all their pantomime civility, they were never far from a bickering match. In fact, before the tournament started, I overheard them going at it. Betty was threatening Gordon, saying she'd tell everyone about his secret."

Claire had overheard similar at the nursing home before the slap.

"What secret was that?"

"She told us Gordon was going to use the morning of the tournament to debut his technology," he replied. "He wanted to dazzle everyone with his inventions. The rest of us agreed that if he did that, we wouldn't stand by him."

Claire mulled over this new piece of the puzzle. Gordon's desire to modernise had been a point of contention within the team since Claire first arrived in the village. In fact, it was the first thing she overheard between Dot and Gordon before they'd even climbed out of the car.

"He couldn't let his micromanaging ways go after he retired," Henry said, sighing. "Like Betty, we should have broken away from Gordon and his control a long time ago." He took one last sip of his tea before throwing the rest into the soil. "We should get back to work. They could release Malcolm any moment and he can't see the place like this."

Henry pushed himself up and pottered off, leaving Claire with more questions than answers. She wasn't sure what to make of the postman. Like Malcolm, he had a shy side. It made their friendship make sense, and Henry was saying all of the right things about wanting the best for Malcolm.

But what if Henry had been the one to bury the bowl in Malcolm's garden? It wasn't like he didn't spend time there. Claire gulped down the rest of the tea, not sure what to think.

She grabbed the rake, ready to dive back into the task at hand, when the rumble of an engine caught her attention. She turned to see Julia's vintage car trundling along the lane, its aqua blue paint gleaming in the sunlight. The car pulled up, and Julia emerged, carrying boxes of cakes.

"I heard what happened," Julia said, looking devastated as she took in the destruction. "I thought you might need some sustenance after all your hard work."

"Oh, Julia, you're an angel," Dot exclaimed, taking the boxes from her. "Thank you so much."

Dot carried the cakes over to Greta, offering her first pick as if they were lifelong friends. The gesture warmed Claire's heart, seeing the two women bond over the shared experience of helping Malcolm.

"The tide seems to have turned for those two," Julia said, nodding at Dot and Greta as they laughed about something.

"Turns out having a common enemy in Gordon and a few hours of garden work does wonders for bonding."

Claire recounted the events that had unfolded in Malcolm's garden—Gordon's rampage, the accusations, and the growing strains within the bowls team.

"The police seem certain they've got their murderer," Claire said. "They were wrong before… do you think Malcolm could be behind the deaths?"

Julia sighed, looking off to the garden.

"Malcolm was a suspect in another murder a few years ago," she said. "Not unlike this one… he didn't used to be the leader of the Peridale Green Fingers. Their leader died and I thought he might have been guilty. Being so quiet and reclusive, it's easy to believe anything you want about him, but I've got to know him over the years. He's become a regular in my cafe, always pottering around the village sprucing up the flowers, litter picking. He's quiet and shy, but well liked, and he's worked hard to build his reputation up after the Green Fingers murder." She met Claire's eyes with a resolute stare. "I don't think he'd resort to such things. Gut feeling."

"I guess time will tell, but speaking of gut feelings, you were right to distrust your gran's alibi."

Julia groaned. "What have you found out?"

"It's nothing bad. When we were walking back from the allotment, Dot finally admitted where she was when Robert was murdered. She left the tournament and went to the nursing home, hoping to drum up new members to join a breakaway team."

"That's all?" Julia forced a laugh, shaking her head in her gran's direction as she and Greta ordered Eugene and Henry around. "Why didn't she just say that?"

"She didn't want the rest of her team to find out she was trying to ditch them. She was hoping to enter whatever team she could scramble together for the second day of the tournament before Gordon was discharged. I think she made it into a bigger deal in her head and clung to her fake alibi. I can go to the nursing home to verify, but I believed her this time."

"That's good enough for me," Julia said with a relieved smile.

"That's Dot, but… how well do you know Henry?"

"Henry's been one of the postmen around the village for as long as I can remember," Julia said, pulling open her creaky car door. "He keeps himself to himself, but he seems nice enough. He pops into the café for a cup of tea now and then, but he's not the chattiest of men. Why do you ask?"

"I overheard Henry muttering something about wishing the poison worked on Gordon earlier," Claire whispered. "I talked to him, and he seems protective about keeping things as they are. Doesn't seem to like anything messing with his routine. What if he… snapped?"

"I don't think he'd try to frame Malcolm though, would he?" Julia said, climbing into her car. She wound the window down and said, "I need to get back to the café, but if you're free for dinner tonight, I'm treating you to something at The Comfy Corner. We can talk more about it then. I may have got us a date with Gordon's new paramedic girlfriend."

CHAPTER SEVENTEEN

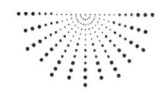

Claire rushed into The Comfy Corner, slightly out of breath after losing track of time in the B&B's garden. As she stepped inside, Mary Todd greeted her with a warm smile.

"Julia's already waiting for you at the bar, love," she said in a knowing whisper. "Whatever you two are up to."

Claire thanked Mary and made her way across the restaurant to the bar, where she found Julia sipping a glass of white wine. The place had a few diners dotted here and there, but it was nowhere near as busy as during Claire's previous visit. A pint of beer sat waiting for Claire, and Julia let out a relieved-sounding breath as Claire approached.

"Hope you don't mind, but I ordered ahead," she said,

sliding the pint towards her. "I guessed you were more of a beer girl than a wine one."

"You guessed correctly," Claire replied, taking a grateful sip. "Sorry I'm late. I got caught up playing hide and seek with the kids. How Amelia thought I'd find her in the compost bin, I'll never know, but she wasn't giving up until I did."

"Some things are worth being late for." She nodded towards a table where her sister, Sue, sat alone. "Speaking of late, Emily should have been here fifteen minutes ago. We might be waiting for nothing."

Sue caught Julia's eye and shrugged, a hint of disappointment on her face.

"How did you manage to set this up?" Claire asked.

"Sue vaguely knows Emily from when she used to work on the wards at the hospital before transferring to the ambulance team," she explained. "Sue is on a sabbatical of sorts from the health field while she works at my café. She convinced Emily to agree to meet her under the guise of asking questions about the switch to the paramedic team."

"Smart cover."

"Except it doesn't seem to have worked." Julia glanced back at Sue, who was now fiddling with her phone. "The only other idea I had was calling for an ambulance and crossing my fingers Emily shows up with it, but I'm not about to waste their time like that when they're as thinly stretched as they are."

Claire leaned in closer to Julia, her voice low. "I've been thinking over what Henry told me earlier."

"Oh?"

"He overheard Betty and Gordon arguing about 'secrets' before the tournament, just like I did at the nursing home. Henry seems to think the secret was about Gordon wanting to debut his technology at the tournament."

"But that doesn't make sense. Everyone already knew about Gordon's plans."

Claire nodded. "Exactly. The more I thought about it while getting ready, the less of a secret it seemed. There has to be something else going on here."

"So, we have Henry admitting to considering poisoning Gordon, an article that potentially inspired the method, and a secret that doesn't quite add up. It's a lot to unpack."

"And let's not forget the missing murder weapon from Malcolm's garden," Claire added.

"It's possible," Julia agreed. "If he was framed, who would want to do that? And why?"

"That's the question, isn't it? We need to figure out what this secret is and how it connects to everything else."

"Well, it looks like Emily isn't going to show. Maybe we should regroup and come up with a new plan."

"You might not have to do anything as drastic," Mary said from across the bar. She seemed to have been eavesdropping on everything. "Don't look now, but if you're waiting for the Emily I think you are, she just came in."

"You know her?" Julia asked.

"Only from her coming in here," Mary said. "I recognise her from all those dates she had with Gordon in Lover's Corner. Seems they started courting as soon as his marriage to Betty fell apart."

"Did you ever overhear anything strange during those dates?" Julia asked, her voice tinged with hope.

"Not really. They were always whispering, and when they weren't whispering, they were bickering. Not a well-suited couple, if you ask me, but she seemed charmed by him."

Claire turned her attention back to the restaurant and spotted Emily taking a seat at the table with Sue. From the moment she sat down, Emily was already checking her watch, perched in a way that looked like she might spring up and leave at any moment.

"What's the plan?" Claire asked, turning to face Julia.

Julia shrugged. "I don't have one. I thought we'd play it by ear."

Without hesitation, Julia took a large swig of her wine and slid off the bar stool. She strode across the mildly busy restaurant with determined strides. As she approached the table, she grabbed two chairs from a nearby table and added them to their setup, the sudden action startling Emily.

Emily's eyes darted between Julia and Claire as they took their seats at the table. The paramedic's suspicious gaze then shifted to Sue.

Sue, uneasy with the entire situation, introduced Julia as her sister and Claire as her sister's friend. Her words were hesitant, as if navigating a minefield.

Emily ignored the introductions, her attention focused solely on Sue.

"What's going on?" she demanded.

Julia, undeterred by Emily's hostility, leaned forward and explained that they had happened to be in the restaurant and wanted to ask her some questions about her involvement with Gordon.

"Why?" Emily retorted, her tone laced with scepticism. She crossed her arms, her body language closing off any attempt at friendly conversation.

"Two people have died, and another was poisoned," Claire said, unable to bite her tongue. "From where I'm standing, you're one of the people in the middle of everything."

"Am I now?" Emily replied, her words measured and

guarded. She revealed nothing, her expression a mask of cool indifference.

Sue shifted uncomfortably in her seat, clearing her throat as if to diffuse the building tension. The air crackled with unspoken accusations and suspicions.

"We were hoping you could shed some light on things," Julia said, adopting a softer approach than Claire's direct confrontation.

"I have nothing to say to you," Emily responded, her eyes narrowing, her lips pressed into a thin line.

"You're being awfully defensive," Claire observed, her words hanging in the air like a challenge.

Emily's glare turned to Claire, fury burning in her eyes. The intensity of her stare spoke volumes, but she remained silent, refusing to engage further.

Claire leaned back in her chair, studying Emily's reactions. The paramedic's defensive demeanour and evasive answers only fuelled Claire's suspicions. She'd been eager to ask about the complex dynamics between the members of the love square, but now her focus narrowed to Emily herself.

Emily reached for a menu and held it up, partially obscuring her face as she pretended to read the options. As she moved, a waft of her perfume drifted towards Claire, triggering a flash of recognition. Bergamot. She'd encountered that scent before in the entrance hall at Wellington Heights.

Claire's mind raced, recalling Betty's words about Emily being her former co-worker and neighbour. For whatever reason, Claire had assumed she'd meant former neighbour as well and hadn't questioned it. She decided to take a chance.

"You live at Wellington Heights, don't you?" she asked, her tone measured but direct.

Emily lowered the menu, her eyes meeting Claire's.

"What of it?"

Julia shifted in her seat, clearly taken aback by this revelation. The air grew thick with tension as Claire pressed on.

"Where were you the morning Betty was poisoned?"

The question hung in the air, demanding an answer.

"Working." But as soon as the word left her lips, her gaze narrowed on Sue. "I thought better of you. Thanks for the ambush."

Emily stood up in a flash, knocking over her chair. The clunk echoed through the dining room, silencing the place. She stormed out of the restaurant, and the door slammed behind her with a resounding thump. The silence that dragged out was broken only by the patter of Mary's feet as she rushed over to pick up the fallen chair.

"She was just as rude last time she was in," she muttered, shaking her head in disapproval.

Claire exchanged a look with Julia, both taken aback

by Emily's abrupt departure. Sue's cheeks burned red, clearly embarrassed by how things had gone.

"I'm sorry," Sue said. "I thought she'd be more willing to talk."

"It's not your fault," Julia reassured her sister, reaching across the table to give her hand a comforting squeeze. "We didn't expect her to react like that. Perhaps we could have built more trust before questioning her about the murders?"

Sue shook her head. "Honestly, I don't think it would have mattered. Emily seemed in a bad mood from the moment she sat down. She mentioned she'd quit her job this morning and wouldn't be much help to me."

"Quit?" Claire echoed, her eyebrows shooting up in surprise. "That's strange timing, don't you think? Did she say why?"

"I didn't get that far before you two joined us."

"Do you think you could find out more about why she quit?" Julia asked. "Claire's right about the timing."

"I'll see what I can find out, but if I've done my part here, I need to get home to put the twins to bed."

As Sue left, Julia and Claire made their way back to the bar, still reeling from their encounter with Emily.

"Well, that was rather unproductive," Julia sighed, slumping onto a bar stool.

Claire, however, wasn't so quick to dismiss the interaction.

"Maybe not," she mused, her fingers tapping thoughtfully against the polished wood of the bar. "I wasn't sure about Emily as a suspect before, but after that display... she must be involved somehow, right? Why else would she react like that?"

"Good point."

Mary approached them, wiping down the bar with a practised hand. Claire seized the opportunity to probe further.

"Mary, earlier you mentioned something about Emily being just as rude the last time she was here. What did you mean by that?"

"It was just last week," Mary paused her cleaning, leaning in conspiratorially. "She came in, insisting on buying a bottle of elderflower cordial."

"Did you sell her a bottle?" Julia asked.

"I don't even stock elderflower cordial," Mary continued. "Can't stand the taste myself, and nobody ever asks for it. But she was so insistent, like it was a matter of life and death."

"Or perhaps life or death," Julia said.

"Do you think..."

"It doesn't mean she poisoned Gordon," Julia said, tipping her head from one side then the other. "If Gordon wasn't drinking, it would make sense that someone bought the cordial. Doesn't mean it was the same person who poisoned it."

"There's another detail," Mary said, glancing around the place. "I didn't think much of it at the time, but hearing you two now... well... perhaps I should have gone to the police right away."

"What is it, Mary?" Julia pushed.

"She was very particular about the bottle it came in," Mary revealed, gulping. "She said it had to be a cork and not a screw top. I asked what difference it made, and she told me to mind my business, so I told her to go elsewhere. Do you think Emily is behind all these killings?"

The question hung in the air, a challenge waiting to be answered.

CHAPTER EIGHTEEN

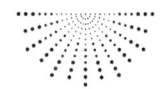

*E*ven later that evening, Claire sat beside Ryan on the edge of Mrs Beaton's bed at Oakwood, the room filled with the gentle hum of the vinyl player spinning old jazz classics in the corner.

"You were such a little fat kid," Mrs Beaton said to Ryan, a smile playing on her lips. "Always running around the cul-de-sac, causing mischief."

"Those were the days, Mrs Beaton."

"And what about my house, dear?" she asked Claire. "When can I come home?"

Claire's heart sank. She'd come to expect the confusion, but it never got easier.

"You put the house up for sale and moved to the Cotswolds, remember?"

"Oh, yes," Mrs Beaton said, her eyes clouding for a moment before clearing again. "Where's Molly?"

Just as Claire was about to try to change the subject, Mrs Beaton's eyes narrowed, a sly smile spreading across her face.

"So, are you two courting now?"

"We are." Claire smiled. "Been a few years already."

"I *always* knew you had eyes for Ryan," she said with a cheeky wink, "even when he ran off to Spain."

Claire's eyebrows drifted up. She hadn't expected Mrs Beaton to remember that detail from so long ago. Ryan squeezed Claire's hand, a warm smile on his face.

"It took me a while to come to my senses," he said, "but I'm glad I did."

"You hold on to each other. Make a proper go of it. Get married, have babies, move in together. Life is short. Life is..." Her gaze wandered around the nursing home room, and a flicker of confusion crossed her face. "Have you seen Molly? Big fat ginger thing. Can't stop her eating, the greedy sod." She looked at Claire again and said, "Are you going to buy my old house?"

"We wanted to, but we can't afford it. It's £50,000 more than any bank will give us." She forced a smile, trying to reassure both Mrs Beaton and herself. "It's okay. We'll figure something out."

Mrs Beaton blinked at Claire, her expression growing distant.

"The nurses here are putting things in my food," she said with a knowing nod. "I keep forgetting things. I reckon my mother put them up to it."

Claire's heart sank as a wave of hopelessness washed over her, but she knew she had to keep the conversation going. An idea sparked in her mind, and she gently touched Mrs Beaton's arm.

"Mrs Beaton, what were your favourite opera songs to sing?" she asked, hoping to steer the conversation to a happier place.

Mrs Beaton's face lit up, her eyes shining with excitement.

"Oh, there were so many!" she exclaimed, her voice filled with joy. "'Casta Diva' from Norma, 'Vissi d'arte' from Tosca, and, of course, 'Un bel dì vedremo' from Madama Butterfly."

As she listed the songs, Mrs Beaton began to sing, her voice growing louder and more confident with each note. She wandered over to the window, staring into the darkness as she poured her heart into the music. Loud banging on the wall coming from the direction of Gordon's room interrupted their peace.

"We should probably get going," Ryan said, glancing at his watch. "It's getting late, and we need to put the kids to bed."

Claire tried to catch Mrs Beaton's attention, but she was too lost in her singing to notice.

"I'll visit again before we head back to Northash, Mrs Beaton," Claire called over the singing, but it went ignored.

Claire pulled the scrapbook from her bag and rested her hand on it. Mrs Beaton had given it to her, but perhaps reading over the stories from the paper, from the beginning of her dazzling career to her eventual 'death at sea', would help. She placed it on her bedside table before they slipped out of the room.

"You know, in some ways, she seems a lot better than when I last saw her back in her filthy house," he started, his voice tinged with both hope and sadness.

"In other ways, she's worse," she finished, grabbing his hand. "That's just the nature of her condition. There's no 'getting better.' It's more like a rollercoaster that sometimes goes up, but always ends up going back down."

"It's hard to see her like this," he admitted, his voice barely above a whisper.

As they passed Gordon's room, the banging on the wall persisted, but Mrs Beaton's singing grew more defiant. Claire knocked on Gordon's door.

"What are you doing?"

"Giving him a piece of my mind."

To Claire's surprise, Gordon called out, "Come in."

She walked in, but the shock on his face revealed he had been expecting someone else. Possibly Emily?

"Get out," he demanded.

"You just invited me in. And you should be kinder to Mrs Beaton."

"Why?" he scoffed.

"Because," she said, "in another twenty-five years, that might be you. Singing makes her happy. It's what she knows. Leave her be."

"You're a good-for-nothing mouthy woman. Go back to where you came from." Gordon's face reddened with anger. "Go on, get out!"

Gordon charged at her, and Claire jumped out of the room before he could get too close, and he slammed the door in her face.

"That was uncalled for!" Ryan cried, banging on the door.

"Gordon..." Feeling emboldened, Claire called through the door, "I know your secret."

She hoped to rattle him into opening up again, but he remained silent. If the bridge between them hadn't already been burned, it was now well and truly destroyed. At least he had stopped banging on Mrs Beaton's wall.

"What is his secret?" he asked.

"No idea." She shrugged. "Maybe I never will, but I seem to have rattled him."

"You're playing with fire, Claire."

"I'm a candlemaker, Ryan," she said, staring ahead at

the end of the corridor as they set off. "Playing with fire comes with the territory."

BACK AT THE B&B, CLAIRE WAS SURPRISED TO FIND JULIA waiting for her in the sitting room, surrounded by Amelia and Hugo, who were giving her tarot readings.

"You're back," Julia said, looking up from the cards spread out before her. "Your children have been keeping me entertained with their tarot skills. Each reading seems to be more ominous than the last. Apparently, my head is going to fall off and all my teeth are going to turn to wood."

"The universe works in mysterious ways," Amelia said.

"Any happy predictions to deliver?" Ryan asked.

"I'm going to win the lottery, too," Julia said with a wink.

"Twice," Hugo reminded her. "In the same day. On a Tuesday."

"I'll have to buy a ticket because my luck seems to have come in," Julia said, standing up from the armchair to join Claire by the door. "I think I have two pieces of good news of my own to deliver."

"Oh?"

"Sue got to the bottom of the situation with Emily,"

she began, her voice lowering. "First, Emily didn't 'quit' her job... they *fired* her."

"Fired? Why?"

"Improper conduct," she replied. "Sue doesn't know any more details beyond that yet, but she said someone will, so she's going to keep digging."

"And the second thing?"

Julia took a deep breath. "Apparently, Emily moved from the hospital wards to the ambulance team because she was having an affair with a senior doctor. A married senior doctor older than her."

"Sounds familiar."

"And here's the kicker." Julia's nostrils flared as she inhaled. "She was *blackmailing* him. Which got me thinking..."

"What if Emily has been blackmailing Gordon?" Claire suggested.

"Exactly. What your dad said about Gordon's poisoning being a warning shot. What if Emily tried to scare Gordon into complying by showing him how serious she was?"

"Mary told us about Emily's search for the elderflower cordial. Being a nurse, she might have known how much would give Gordon a reaction without killing him."

"There's a pattern of manipulation and deceit there," Julia said, her eyes sparkling with the thrill of the investigation. "We might be onto something here."

"What if..." she began, her voice hushed with the weight of her theory. "What if Emily manipulated her way into Gordon's will, like people said Betty did with Robert? And..." A jigsaw piece slotted into place. "She killed Betty to make sure she had no other competition at the time of the will reading? Even Betty wasn't sure if she was still in Gordon's will."

"But what about Robert?" Julia asked, furrowing her brow. "Why would Emily target him?"

Claire chewed over the question for a moment, several theories swirling.

"Robert used to be Gordon's close friend, right?" Claire started. "What if he found out something about Emily's plan and wanted to warn Gordon?"

"Or what if Robert was in Gordon's will with—"

"Ladies?" Ryan called, beckoning them over to the bay window. "You'll want to see this."

They hurried over and joined Ryan at the window. Across the street, Malcolm and Henry were locked in an embrace under the glow of the streetlamp. DI Moyes watched on from the station door, sending smoke into the night.

"Even with the murder weapon in his garden, they couldn't charge him," Julia said in a small voice. "I think it's safe to say he's innocent."

"Which doesn't leave many people left in the frame,"

Claire agreed. "Think Malcolm will be in the mood to talk?"

"Only one way to find out."

Side by side, they made their way out of the B&B and crossed the street. As they approached, Malcolm and Henry parted from their hug, both looking the most relieved Claire had seen them since before Gordon's poisoning.

"A free man, at last," Claire began, her voice gentle. "We're glad to see you're out, Malcolm. How are you holding up?"

Malcolm shrugged, holding back a quivering yawn.

"As well as expected, I suppose. It's been a trying few days."

"Ladies, we've been through enough already," Henry said, firmer than Claire had heard him. "If you're about to launch into another of your interrogations, please can it wait until—"

Claire held up a hand. "We're not here to cause any trouble. We have a theory about who might be behind all of this, and we were hoping you could help us."

"What's your theory?" Malcolm asked.

"We think it might be Emily, the paramedic," Julia said. "She's been involved with Gordon, and we believe she might be blackmailing him. Do either of you know her well?"

"Not outside of her being Gordon's girlfriend," Henry

said, folding his arms. "Why do you think it could be her?"

Claire explained their suspicions about Emily's motives, including her potential manipulation of Gordon's will and her desire to eliminate any threats to her inheritance. Coupled with the elderflower cordial, her medical knowledge, and her blow-up at The Comfy Corner, Malcolm and Henry looked as convinced as Julia and Claire.

"It sounds like a credible theory," Malcolm admitted. "Gordon latched onto Emily as soon as he found out about Betty and Robert. And if it's not me, and it's not Henry, and it's not Dot… who else?"

"But how are you going to prove it?" Henry asked. "If she wasn't willing to answer a few questions over dinner, she's not going to confess to murder."

"We haven't got that far," Julia admitted.

Claire's mind raced as she tried to formulate a plan. Henry was right. There was no way Emily would confess, and she was reminded of her conversation with her father. What had he said he'd done when he'd known the real Northash Strangler would never confess?

"We need to catch her in the act," Claire remembered aloud.

"Catch her committing another murder?" Julia asked, sounding as unsure as Malcolm and Henry looked. "But… how?"

Claire scanned their surroundings and landed on the glowing red tip of DI Moyes' vape lighting up the dark as the detective puffed her clouds.

"I think I might have an idea," Claire said, biting back a grin. "Can I treat you to a pint at the pub, fellas? I think we're going to need all hands-on deck for this one." When they nodded, she said, "Find a table and I'll meet you in there. I need to make a quick phone call."

Malcolm and Henry followed Julia across the road to the hazy glow of The Plough. Claire followed a few steps behind, pulling out her phone. She called her parents' home phone, glad when her dad was the one to pick up.

"Evening, little one. How's things?"

"By tomorrow, I think they'll be better," she said, turning to take in the empty village green in the distance. "But before then, I need to ask you some more questions about your old Northash Strangler case, and more specifically, the trap that you set…"

CHAPTER NINETEEN

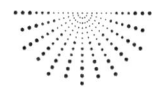

*C*laire tossed and turned throughout the night, unable to find peace amidst her swirling thoughts about their plan. When morning finally arrived, she picked at her breakfast, her appetite nowhere to be found. She was the furthest from hungry she had ever been, unable to eat more than a few bites.

In the café kitchen, Julia pushed a steaming cup of black coffee into Claire's hands with a smile.

"I've put an extra shot in there for you."

Claire returned the smile.

"Thanks. You're reminding me of Damon, my friend who I work with at the candle shop back home. We start our mornings with a fresh coffee. We can always tell when the other needs an extra shot. Usually because one of us has had one too many pints of homebrew at The

Hesketh." She stared at the black surface, her tired expression reflecting back at her. "I'm craving that normalcy right now."

"You can be on the road back home this afternoon if you want," Julia said in a soft, reassuring voice. "Back to Damon and your candle shop and your cats."

"And my mother," Claire said with a laugh. "That said, I've had my fill with your gran. They'd be scrapping like two alley cats if they ever ended up in the same room."

"There's still time." Julia chuckled. "I wouldn't mind coming to see this Northash of yours one day."

"Really?" Claire sipped her coffee. "You'd always be welcome."

"Really. I need to come and visit my new friend, don't I?" She nudged their shoulders together. "And maybe next time, we won't find ourselves in the middle of a mess like this."

"These sorts of messes seem to find me."

"Yeah, me too." Julia laughed and Claire joined in. "Just can't ever seem to behave myself."

"What's that old saying? 'Well-behaved women rarely make history'?"

"I'm not trying to make history—I just like to see things set right. Like a perfect recipe."

"Or a candle fragrance." Claire lifted her cup and clinked it against the edge of Julia's sweet and minty smelling tea. "To setting things right."

Claire took another sip of her coffee, willing the extra shot of espresso to give her a much-needed jolt of energy. They were interrupted by a knock at the back door. Julia set down her tea and went across the kitchen to answer it. She opened the door to Henry in his red postman uniform, and he peered around Julia, nodding a greeting at Claire. She noticed his knobbly knees clacking together more than the slight chill in the air warranted.

He opened his postal bag and showed Julia something.

"I've got them," he said. "Do you want them in here?"

"Take them to my gran's cottage across the green. Barker and Ryan are there to get everything set up, and they know what to do next."

"Won't it look suspicious?"

"You're a postman, Henry," Julia assured him. "People expect you to be delivering things."

"Right."

"Did you deliver the letter to Wellington Heights?"

"I did," he said. "Wrote it in red ink, just like you asked. Unmarked envelope, and signed 'from Dot.' I've… I've never done anything like this before."

"None of us have," Julia said, patting him on the shoulder. "Don't worry. After today, this will all be over and things can go back to normal. We don't have much time."

"Right." He stepped back, taking another peep into his bag. "Back to normal. That's all I want."

Henry left, and Julia resumed drinking her tea against the counter. They stood in silence for a moment, the only sounds filling the space between their slurps coming from the busy village green outside.

"All we can do now is wait and see if Emily shows up," Claire said.

"If Emily is as guilty as we think she is," Julia stated, "she will."

Malcolm emerged through the beaded curtain separating the café from the kitchen, his hands trembling as he approached. His glass, once filled with water, was now empty.

"Could I get a refill, please?" Malcolm asked, his voice quivering. "I... I know I wasn't supposed to drink it, but..."

Julia nodded, her expression soft with understanding. She took the glass from Malcolm's unsteady hands and retrieved a filtered water jug from the fridge. As she filled the glass, Malcolm's hands continued to shake, even as he tried to steady them against the counter.

"How are you feeling?" Claire asked. "Better after a night in your own bed?"

"I didn't get much sleep," he admitted. He took a small sip of water, his eyes downcast. "My mind was too busy churning with everything that's happened."

"I know the feeling. Neither did we," Claire said.

Malcolm managed a faint smile at that, but he still seemed shaken by the ordeal. Claire couldn't blame him.

To be arrested and questioned over two murders when you were innocent...

"Everyone out there is staring at me," he said, glancing back at the empty café. "They all still think I'm guilty. This is worse than last time."

"That will work to our advantage," Julia said. "After today, nobody will think that anymore."

"I know it's been awful, Malcolm," Claire added. "But it will be over soon. All of it."

Malcolm managed a weak smile again, but it didn't reach his eyes.

"I hope so. I just want things to go back to normal. Back to my garden, my routine..." He trailed off, staring off into the corner of the room. "Are we doing the right thing? And why does it have to be me?"

"Everything will go according to plan, Malcolm." Julia handed him the refilled glass, her voice gentle but firm. "We've thought this through."

"It has to be you, Malcolm, because Emily tried to frame you," Claire said. "She must have been the one to plant the murder weapon in your garden. She had everyone believing you could be a murderer, so why not use that to our advantage?"

"We need to make it plausible that you might strike again, or she might not take the bait," Julia added, letting her words sink in. "Emily's come this far to keep her crimes hidden. She thinks she's untouchable. Why wouldn't she fall for another opportunity to silence someone else threatening to reveal her secrets?"

Malcolm took a sip of water, his grip tightening around the glass as if seeking comfort in its solidity.

"I'm not supposed to drink it," he said, lowering the glass. "Will she mind when I...?"

"My gran?" Julia laughed. "Despite what she says, she loves the drama and wouldn't turn down the opportunity for a little performance in front of the whole village." In a cheerier voice, she said, "So, how are things looking out on the green?"

"There are more people than last time. It seems all the chaos has drawn the biggest crowd the tournament has ever seen." He glanced over his shoulder again. "Gordon's here, too. He's showing off his box of tricks, trying to drum up interest in his inventions with the other teams."

"I need to see this," Claire said, taking a gulp of her coffee. "I'd be lying if I said I wasn't curious to know what all the fuss was about."

Claire stepped out into the bright sunshine bathing the green, though dark clouds peppered the horizon behind the church. Gordon stood on the edge of the green while teams engaged in practice rounds before the tournament. A few people gathered around to watch his display, but most had their backs to him. He spread his arms like an old-fashioned salesman trying to peddle snake oil to the crowd, and he might as well have been, given the lack of interest.

"This *is* the future of our beloved sport," Gordon announced, holding up a bowl. "I have rightfully taken it where no man has taken this game before. Each ball isn't just a ball; it has technology built into the fabric. Proximity sensors and lasers take the guesswork out. No more tape measures to see whose bowl gets further."

He demonstrated with a simple throw, and the bowl rolled across the green towards the yellow target bowl. A second throw got another bowl closer to the yellow, and a ring around the middle flashed green as a little victory tune played from within. A few people looked impressed, most shaking their heads in irritation.

"And you don't need to waste your energy bending down to pick them up," he continued, producing a small remote control. With a click of a button, all the bowls rolled back to him, causing people to jump out of the way. "My invention gives you full control over every aspect of the game."

Gordon seemed impressed with himself, but his audience appeared perplexed, clearly not interested.

"I've used decades of experience to come up with the perfected version of the game," he said desperately, but people turned their backs on him, walking away from his demonstration. "This really *is* the future. You don't have to agree, but it is…"

"Henry was right," Claire said to Julia. "Gordon is trying to suck out the spirit of the game. No wonder his team turned against him."

Out of the corner of her eye, Claire saw Greta and Eugene hurrying down the street, panting for breath but not slowing down. They went back into the café, where Amelia and Hugo were being kept entertained by Evelyn reading their tea leaves.

"Emily is on her way from Wellington Heights," Greta announced.

"And she looks *furious*," Eugene added, dabbing his red face with his pocket square. "It looked like she had the letter in her hand, too."

"We had to take a shortcut to get back before her." Greta leaned against her knees, inhaling a deep breath. "That's got me warmed up for the tournament."

Claire's heart raced at the news. This was it—the moment they had been waiting for. She glanced at Julia, who nodded in silent understanding. They had to act fast.

"Malcolm, it's time," Claire said, turning to the nervous man. "Remember, just stick to the plan, and everything will be fine."

Malcolm swallowed hard, his hands trembling as he gripped the glass of water.

"I... I don't know if I can do this."

"You can," Julia assured him, placing a comforting hand on his shoulder. "You're just having a little stage fright. We'll be right there with you, every step of the way."

Malcolm left, and Claire and Julia exchanged worried glances, uncertainty hanging heavy in the air.

"Is there a chance we're wrong?" Claire asked, her voice barely above a whisper.

"We can't be wrong. It *has* to be her. Gordon has his alibi, and the rest are dead. It's either Emily, Malcolm, or Henry at this point."

"And if the police couldn't charge Malcolm based on finding a murder weapon in his garden, then we can pretty much rule him out, right?"

"What did you just say?" Henry said, returning from Dot's at that very moment.

"I'm sorry, Henry." Julia turned to him, an apologetic look on her face. "I don't think it was you either, but based on the evidence alone, I can't fully rule you out."

"No, before that," Henry insisted, his eyes narrowing. "Something about an alibi. Gordon's alibi."

Claire's heart skipped a beat. "Yes, Gordon's alibi. He was discharged from the hospital after Robert was murdered."

Henry fell silent, his expression pensive as he seemed to be piecing together a puzzle in his mind. Before anyone could press him further, Greta's urgent whisper cut through the tension.

"She's *coming!*" Greta hissed, her nose pressed against the glass alongside Eugene's. "The killer is on the loose!"

Claire hurried to join them at the window, her heart pounding in her chest. Through the glass, she watched as Emily strode purposefully towards the green, scanning the crowd as if searching for someone specific. To her surprise, instead of approaching Dot, who was throwing practice bowls with her new team composed of familiar-looking nursing home residents and Percy, Emily cut past them and made a beeline for Gordon, who was packing up his box near the car. She leaned in close, whispering something to him that Claire couldn't quite make out from a distance.

As planned, a commotion erupted on the green, drawing everyone's attention. Dot and Malcolm were engaged in a heated argument, their voices rising above the chatter. Malcolm, shaking off his timid manner, was attempting to assert his right to lead the team, while Dot vehemently insisted that she had formed a new team and that Malcolm would not be a part of it, given his status as a suspected murderer.

In a shocking turn of events, Malcolm, his frustration boiling over, threw the glass of water he had been clutching directly into Dot's face. Gasps of disbelief rippled through the gathered crowd, and Dot, her face dripping and mouth agape, let out a mighty roar before she stormed across the green towards her cottage. Percy scurried behind her, struggling to keep up with her furious pace.

"Everything's going according to plan," Julia said. "Now we just need to wait for—"

The cottage door slammed shut, and a moment later, the back door of the café burst open. They all turned around to see Sue rushing in, out of breath.

"Julia, why do you always have your phone on silent?" Sue chastised her sister.

"What's going on?" Julia checked her phone and Claire saw a list of missed calls. "I'm sorry, it's a work habit, and—"

"I went back to the hospital to keep digging into what happened with Emily," Sue explained, catching her breath. "There's always someone who has the dirt, and I got it from one of the long-timer nurses, Brenda. She knew why Emily was fired."

"Why?" Claire asked.

"She was fired for having a patient's records tampered with," Sue revealed. "Altered."

"But how could she do that?" Julia questioned. "She was a paramedic."

"Remember that senior doctor I told you Emily was having an affair with? She was also extorting him. Brenda heard from Marge, whose cousin is a doctor in the same department as Emily's fancy man, that Emily was blackmailing him. For money," Sue explained, taking another deep breath. "Cough up, or else Emily would tell his wife about what he was getting up to in dark corners of the hospital with Emily while his wife was at home looking after their kids."

"Where's this going, Sue?" Julia asked, peeking at the window. "Everything is about to kick off—"

"Trust me, I'm getting there." Leaning in, Sue whispered, "According to Brenda, the doctor paid Emily off under the condition that she 'go away.' That's why she transferred to the ambulance unit. But Emily went back and extorted him one last time, convincing him to alter discharge records of a patient to make it seem like they were discharged hours *after* they actually were."

"Whose records?" Claire asked, already knowing the answer.

"I couldn't find that part out," Sue admitted. "But the doctor she was extorting, his wife left him anyway because Emily wasn't the only nurse he was messing around with, so he had nothing to lose. That's when he went to the board, told them what Emily was up to, and that's why she was fired."

Claire turned to Henry, her eyes widening with realisation.

"Gordon's alibi..." she began, her voice trailing off as the pieces started to fall into place.

"I *saw* them," he said, his expression grave.

Claire remembered what Henry had told her when

they'd paused for tea while clearing Malcolm's garden. Before the tournament, he had witnessed Betty and Gordon arguing about 'Gordon's secret.' But Claire had assumed the argument had taken place sometime before the tournament—perhaps days, weeks, or even months prior.

"I saw them *that* morning," Henry clarified, his voice low. "I heard Gordon had recovered quickly, so I didn't think anything of it when I saw him in the white tent with Betty that morning. I'd heard he'd been discharged later that night after Robert was killed, but I didn't give it a second thought. I wasn't thinking like that, I…"

"Most people wouldn't," Claire assured him.

"He was discharged *that* morning," Sue said, "hours before Robert was murdered. And Brenda let me look at his charts. Yes, he had foxglove poison in his system, but not enough to kill him. Not enough to kill a cat, I'd say. A bad case of heartburn at best."

"But enough to show up in a test," Claire added.

"We got it all wrong," Julia said, shaking her head. "I was so certain…"

"Not all wrong," Claire corrected. "I still think Emily poisoned Gordon, just not in the way we thought."

As planned, the deafening alarm sounded from Dot's cottage across the green. With no more time to waste, Claire followed Julia across the green, hopping over people playing bowls. The whirring alarm filled the air, urging them to hurry. Julia thrust open the front door and Claire followed her into a traditionally decorated hallway. They found Ryan and Barker wrestling Gordon against the stairs as he tried to wriggle away. Dot and Percy watched from the top, struggling to keep their dogs back. The back door stood wide open, and one of Gordon's laser trip wires beamed red across the carpet.

"I was just trying to use the bathroom!" Gordon insisted, his voice strained as he fought against Ryan and Barker's grip.

"No, you weren't." Julia stepped forward, her eyes narrowed. "Of course you're the one behind all of this."

"I have an alibi!" Gordon protested.

"No, you don't." Claire moved past the laser wire, the alarm still ringing in her ears. She closed the back door with a thud, cutting off any potential escape route. Turning to face Gordon, she said, "And you have a lot of explaining to do."

CHAPTER TWENTY

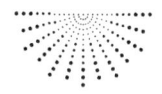

The rain pounded against the windowpane in Dot's dining room, a space that seemed frozen in time with its ornate dark wood furniture, floral wallpaper, and every surface adorned with family photographs. At the centre of the room, Gordon sat alone on one side of the dining table, his jaw set in a defiant clench. Across from him, Claire and Julia occupied the other side, both staring ahead at the man before them—Gordon's eyes were fixed on the rain dribbling down the glass.

Dot leaned against the mantelpiece behind Claire and Julia, her eyes darting between Gordon and the two women, while Malcolm and Henry sat on a small sofa beneath the window, the sound of the rain pelting the garden outside filling the momentary silence. Ryan and

Barker stood guard by the door, ready and waiting for an attempted escape. Behind them, the wispy tendrils of DI Moyes' vape smoke drifted down the hallway.

Claire clasped her hands together on the table.

"You might want to start talking," she said. "We know."

"You've all got the wrong end of the stick," Gordon replied, his voice strained. "If you'll just let me explain—"

"Explain how *I'm* behind all of this?" Malcolm interjected, timid no longer. "Or perhaps you're going to try to pin this on Henry next?"

"I *saw* you, Gordon," Henry stated, nodding in the direction of the village green. "When you should have been in hospital, when we all thought someone had tried to poison you, I saw you here, in the village."

"I was feeling better, so I... I went for a stroll, and then returned to the hospital."

"The hospital is miles away," Julia retorted, shaking her head. "You'd never have got back there in time, and even if you did, that would still cast doubt over your alibi. The truth is, you were discharged early that morning. After tests through the night, doctors saw no reason to keep you in."

"You all saw me after I drank the elderflower cordial," Gordon argued, his voice rising. "Elderflower cordial that was poisoned with foxglove flowers. I almost died!"

Claire could see the desperation in his eyes, the way his hands clenched and unclenched on the table. His usual stench of blind confidence and pig-headed arrogance now mingled with a new scent—fear.

"Elderflower cordial that came in a corked bottle," Claire stated carefully. "A bottle that could easily be opened and closed by anyone at any time, the poison added to it."

"Exactly," Gordon said, his voice tinged with a hint of relief.

Claire shook her head. "We know Emily was on the lookout for such a bottle of elderflower cordial. She must have poisoned the drink."

"*Exactly!*" Gordon repeated. "Emily poisoned me. She must have."

"Yes, she must have," Claire agreed. "Being a nurse, disgraced or not, it wouldn't have been difficult for her to add just the right amount of poison to show up in your system. Just enough that when you keeled over on the green, everyone would think you were poisoned."

Gordon laughed at the suggestion, a forced sound that echoed in the room.

"I claim not to know the complex inner workings of a woman's mind," he said. "Emily has always been troubled."

"Drop the performance, Gordon," Dot interjected. She leaned through Claire and Julia and slapped the polished wood with her palm. "I should have known it was a sham from the moment you fell to the ground. Your acting was amateur at best."

Gordon let out another laugh, but it rang hollow.

"And why would I want to fake being poisoned when I actually was poisoned?" he cried. "That's absurd!"

Claire leaned closer, her eyes locking with Gordon's.

"Exactly," she said, her voice steady. "Absurd enough that none of us ever questioned your alibi. Not once." She paused for a defence that didn't materialise. "You, with the help of your paramedic girlfriend, concocted a plan to make yourself look like the first failed victim of a serial killer. To give you the perfect alibi."

Gordon's jaw clenched, his knuckles whitening as his hands clenched tighter together as panic flooded his darting eyes.

Claire leaned back in her chair, her eyes never leaving Gordon's face. She could see the cracks in his façade, the way his anger was barely concealing his fear.

"Is that what your secret was that Betty knew?" Claire asked, her voice calm and even. "Did she put the pieces together before anyone else after seeing you up and about in the village when you claimed to be in the hospital? Is that why you poisoned her when she visited the nursing home?"

Gordon's fist slammed against the table, the sound echoing through the room.

"*I* didn't poison Betty!" he shouted, his emphasis on the 'I' ringing clear.

"Perhaps not," Julia said, "but Emily lives at Wellington Heights, just like Betty. So you put her up to it."

Another slam of his fist, this time accompanied by a guttural cry of frustration.

"I didn't put her up to *that*!" Gordon yelled, the emphasis on 'that' causing a collective intake of breath. "I mean… I…"

The room fell silent, the burden of Gordon's words settling over them like a heavy blanket. He stared down at the shiny surface of the table, his eyes unfocused, as if he were seeing something far away. The only sound was the steady patter of rain against the window.

"You concocted this complicated plan," Claire said, unwavering, "as complicated as your new game of bowls, so that you could kill Robert. Not with poison, but with the sheer brute force of a blow to the head, with a bowl that you dumped in Malcolm's garden. A bowl that you struck over Robert's head to once and for all get your own back on a man you once called a friend. A man who took your job, took your wife, and was now trying to take your bowls team."

As the words left her lips, Claire watched as Gordon's defiant front crumbled. His shoulders slumped, the fight draining from his eyes as he realised his carefully constructed alibi had fallen apart. Gordon took a deep, shuddering breath before clearing his throat.

"Robert took *everything* from me," he began, his voice low and bitter. "He didn't deserve that promotion. He wasn't as innovative. And he didn't deserve to take over the bowls team. He only joined because I joined. He used to make fun of it. Said it was barely a sport and an excuse for retired nobodies to stand around chatting."

"That's why we enjoy it," Henry said. "That's the point of the game, Gordon. People our age... there's so little for us to do."

Claire watched as Gordon's shoulders sunk further, as he seemed to be reliving the events that had led to this moment.

"But it could have been so much *more*," Gordon said, sighing. "I knew it was only a matter of time before Robert took over the team. Forced me out. Turned everyone against me."

"No such plan was in place," Dot said. "If anything, *I* was the one who was going to stage a coup against you. Robert wasn't the problem, Gordon. *You* were. All your controlling and pushing... it was sucking the fun out of the team." She fixed Gordon with a steely gaze. "You're not even a good bowls player. You're just good at taking control."

"That's what all this was really about, wasn't it?" Julia said. "Control. Control of your wife, a woman you lost years ago through your own neglect of her emotions. A woman who felt so unloved that she turned to a man who had time to listen to her."

"They only held hands," Claire said, "but that was probably more than you had done with her in years. The bowls team might have been the straw that broke the camel's back, but that was just your way to rationalise how hurt you were."

"You tried to keep calm and carry on," Julia said, "keep things civil for appearances' sake, but inside, your resentment was boiling."

"And it bubbled over."

"But you're clearly a smart man."

"Smart enough to create those inventions," Claire said. "Misplaced, but still impressive. If only you'd put those brains to use somewhere else. Instead, you used them to cook up a plan that would leave you out of the frame for murdering Robert in cold blood."

DI Moyes stepped through Barker and Ryan, the wispy tendrils of her vape smoke trailing behind her. The detective's eyes were fixed on Gordon, her expression a mix of triumph and disgust.

"And that's where Emily comes in," DI Moyes stated. "My officers have had a nice chat with her, and she's confessed everything. Confessed to staging the elderflower poisoning under your instruction, Gordon. Confessed to planting the bottle at the café and then taking it before anyone could find it. And... she's confessed to poisoning Betty when Betty figured out that your alibi was a smoke and mirrors show."

Gordon's face twisted into a scowl, his fists clenching on the table.

"I *never* told Emily to murder Betty," he restated, his voice rising with each word. "She was foolish for that. Too gung-ho, always getting ahead of herself. Thought she was clever, but she wasn't. She was easy to... to..."

His words trailed off, the implication hanging heavy in the air. Claire watched as Gordon looked around the room, as if searching for an escape route. But there was none. The truth was out, and there was no turning back.

DI Moyes took a step closer to the table, her eyes never leaving Gordon's face.

"Easy to manipulate?" she suggested, her voice dripping with sarcasm.

Gordon's jaw clenched, his nostrils flaring as he glared up at the detective. But he said nothing, his silence speaking volumes.

"What did you promise her?" Claire asked.

"She already got enough out of me," he spat. "We met at a funeral, and she made it her mission to seduce me. Apparently, she had a thing for older married men and enjoyed entangling herself and exploiting them." He paused, his chest heaving with barely contained rage.

"She was exploiting me. I was paying the rent on her Wellington Heights flat, keeping her in the lap of luxury."

"She must have had something against you?" Julia suggested. "According to Betty, it was your affair with Emily that finally ended your marriage, not her emotional affair, so it wasn't that."

"The plan," he said, his chest deflating. "That night, I saw Betty and Robert whispering in a quiet corner. Smiling. Laughing. Holding hands... I'd been noticing it for a few months. She thought I was blind to it. I suppose I was—it had been going on for years by then." He clenched his eyes shut. "I'd had one too many to drink... I was an idiot, and I told Emily I was going to kill that man. No matter how much I convinced her I hadn't meant it, it didn't matter. She said she'd tell everyone... that she'd go to the police... I told her she should. Who'd believe her?" He dropped his head and heaved out a laugh. "When I started saying 'strange things', she started recording on her phone. She had me right where she wanted me, so I had to turn things around. Over time, she let the mask slip. She had me all to herself. I could tell she had fallen in love with me, or whatever she thought love was." A cold smile lifted his lips. "It didn't take much to convince her I'd be so much happier without Robert. I told her we'd move away, have a fresh start somewhere new, and I'd take her with me. It's like she'd been waiting her whole life to do something like this... when I read that article in the gardening magazine, everything clicked."

"Of course," Claire said with an exhausted sigh. "The murder of Nigella Lawson claims even more victims. She was murdered by her estranged spouse, all because of jealousy and resentment."

"And Nigella's killer almost got away with it. They just needed a better alibi. With Emily's medical knowledge and route to getting access to hospital records, the plan wrote itself. She helped me sneak out of the hospital early that morning, and she stayed behind to make sure she could have the discharge records cooked up by her contact. I waited near that tent until Robert was alone in there..." He clenched his fist. "He was surprised to see me, but he didn't see what I was about to do coming. He thought he had everything under wraps. That team was as good as his. I picked up a bowl and I hit him. He fell to the ground, and that was it." His twisted smile returned, this time taking over his face. "The man who'd been ruining my life was dead, and I was the one who killed him. In the weeks leading up to that moment, I'd spend hours trying to imagine how I'd feel. Regretful, powerful..." He looked up at Claire, and the smile grew. "Do you want to know how I felt? *Satisfied*."

"I've heard enough," DI Moyes said, unhooking a pair of handcuffs from her waistband. "Gordon Wicks, you are under arrest for the murder of Robert Richards and the conspiracy to murder Betty Fletcher."

With a swift motion, DI Moyes secured them around Gordon's wrists. Barker stepped forward, assisting the detective in lifting Gordon from his chair. Despite the gravity of the situation, Gordon's smile lingered.

"You were so focused on Robert... the man who 'ruined' your life," Claire said, "but the man who ruined your life is standing right in front of me. *You*, Gordon. And now you're going to spend the rest of it behind bars."

"Sounds like justice to me," Dot said, dusting her hands together. "Your reign of control has come to an end."

As the words sank in, Gordon's smirk faded, replaced by a look of dawning realisation. DI Moyes and Barker dragged him away, his feet shuffling against the floor. The room exhaled a collective breath.

Julia turned to Claire with a relieved smile. "You did it. Well done."

"*We* did it." Claire glanced out the window at the bright sunshine. "Now, it looks like the shower has passed. Don't we have a bowls tournament to finish?"

CHAPTER TWENTY-ONE

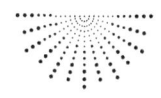

The village green came alive once again as teams from across the Cotswolds gathered to compete in the twice-postponed second day of the tournament. Northash faced off against the likes of Chipping Norton, Stow-on-the-Wold, and Bourton-on-the-Water, their skills put to the test with every round.

Despite their best efforts, Northash found themselves knocked out in the semi-final, a heart-breaking loss that left Claire and her team feeling deflated. However, their spirits lifted as they cheered on the newly formed Peridale team, composed of Dot, Percy, Malcolm, and Henry.

The Peridale team fought valiantly, their determination and teamwork shining through as they advanced to the final. Their opponents, a formidable team from Moreton-in-Marsh, proved to be fierce competitors. The tension mounted as the final throw approached, the outcome of the tournament hanging in the balance.

With bated breath, Claire watched as Malcolm stepped up to take the crucial shot. The crowd fell silent, all eyes fixed on the green. Malcolm took a deep breath, steadied his hand, and released the bowl. It glided across the grass, curving gracefully towards the jack. For a moment, it seemed as though victory was within reach.

But fate had other plans. The bowl from Moreton-in-Marsh, thrown with precision and skill, nudged Malcolm's bowl aside at the last second, securing their triumph. The Peridale team's dreams of lifting the trophy were dashed, but their heads remained high, proud of their incredible journey.

As the tournament drew to a close, Claire found herself at Julia's café, surrounded by the Northash and Peridale teams. The aroma of freshly brewed coffee and the warmth of camaraderie filled the air. Dot and Greta, once rivals, now sat together, sharing stories and laughter over steaming cups of tea. Eugene had struck up a lively conversation with Malcolm and Henry, the three men grinning and chuckling as they shared stories.

In the end, it didn't matter who raised the trophy in the air.

They'd had fun, and by the end of their last game,

Claire was starting to see the appeal. She wasn't sure she was going to join one of the local teams back home anytime soon, but maybe one day... in a few decades.

In the café's kitchen, Claire hugged her coffee while watching Julia whip up a cake batter without having to so much as glance at the handwritten recipe book open on the counter.

"It's incredible how jealousy and resentment can drive people to such extremes," Julia said, dipping her finger against the wooden spoon for a taste. She sprinkled in more sugar and added, "Gordon had every right to be upset about what happened between Betty and Robert, but I can't help but feel an open conversation might have brushed a lot of the dirt under the carpet."

"That would have meant letting go," Claire said, sipping her coffee. "Something Gordon didn't seem able to do. For a man so focused on the future when it came to his lasers, he let his obsession with past mistakes take over."

As they pondered the case, while the cheer in the café rose to dizzying levels—from the sounds of it, Dot and Greta seemed to be holding court—DI Moyes slipped into the kitchen through the back door.

"Gordon and Emily have been charged based on their confessions and the evidence gathered," she said. "Gordon tried to backtrack again, but we got his confession on tape in the end. Emily seems relieved it's all over."

"And the rest of us," Claire said, toasting her cup. "Did she say what drove her to go along with Gordon's murder plan?"

Moyes shook her head. "Not exactly, but I got her to open up about her past. Her dad abandoned her when she was five. I'm no psychologist, but I'd say that might have set her up for a lifetime of difficult relationships with older men. She seems remorseful about poisoning Betty."

"That's something, I suppose," Julia said.

"It seems the fog is clearing, and she's realised just how far she took things. If only Betty hadn't confronted Gordon about her theory." Moyes sighed. "If Emily hadn't acted alone on that one, she might have got away with accessory charges. As it stands, she's not likely to be a free woman until she's Gordon's age. Gordon, on the other hand, he's going to die behind bars."

"Small mercies," Claire said.

"I have to ask," DI Moyes said, leaning against the counter as Julia poured the batter into a cake tin. "How did you manage to catch Gordon in the act?"

Julia grinned and nudged Claire with her elbow.

"It was all Claire's idea. Go on, tell her."

"Actually, you gave me the idea, detective. Well, the red glowing tip of your vape did."

Moyes arched a brow. "Oh?"

"It reminded me of the lasers Gordon had around that patch of land next to Malcolm's cottage. I knew we'd have to catch Emily in the act to prove beyond doubt that it was her. So, we forged a letter from Dot, telling Emily that Dot knew the truth about what happened to Betty and Robert. If Emily didn't pay her £10,000, Dot was going to go to the police."

Julia chuckled. "My gran, of course, volunteered herself immediately, and as it turned out, the blackmailer wasn't one to be blackmailed. She fell for the trap but reported back to the man in charge of everything."

"We had Malcolm and Dot have a public confrontation," Claire continued, "leaving no doubt about where Dot would be at that moment. For all his experience working with lasers, Gordon didn't notice the one waiting for him in Dot's hallway when he went in to strike her down."

"Where Barker and Ryan were waiting in the shadows to grab him before he could cause any more harm," Julia added.

"Clever. Dangerous, but clever." She smiled at Claire. "I'm impressed, Claire."

"It was a team effort."

"Next time, let me in on the team," Moyes said, more to Julia. "You're lucky someone called the station about the altercation between Malcolm and your gran, or I might not have been around to catch Emily before she made a run for it." She checked her watch, pulling open the back door. "All's well that ends well, I suppose. I'll catch you later. I've been promising Roxy I'd take her out for a meal every night this week, but this case has been in the way. Think the Comfy Corner will have a free table?"

"Mary will always squeeze you in," Julia said. "And let her know her information about the cork bottle helped us unravel the case. She'll be as pleased as punch. Have a Peridale pie on me."

"I think I'll pass," Moyes said with a wink. "They're gross."

Moyes left through the back door, and Claire couldn't help but agree with her, though she kept that to herself.

"You should be proud of yourself, Claire. You cracked this case wide open."

Claire shook her head, a modest grin playing on her lips. "I was just doing what my dad would have done."

"Don't sell yourself short." Julia placed a hand on Claire's shoulder. "Take the credit. You're brilliant on your own, and you proved that today."

"Thank you, but I couldn't have done it without your help. We make a pretty good team."

Julia laughed. "That we do. Who knows, maybe we should make this a regular thing?"

Claire chuckled at the thought. "I think I'll stick to making candles for now. But if another mystery comes knocking, you know where to find me."

"Given how often that seems to happen around here," Julia said, leaning in, "you might just regret saying that."

Claire followed Julia back into the café, a sense of pride swelling in her chest. The celebration was in full swing, with laughter and chatter filling the air. She made her way to Ryan and the children, who were seated at a table near the window, their faces alight with joy.

"I can see thunder and lightning," Amelia said as she swirled the dregs in a teacup around, "and *explosions!*"

"I see a dinosaur," Hugo said, shrugging.

"But Evelyn said *I* had the sight."

"Then maybe it's time for an eye test," Ryan said, pulling out a chair for Claire. "Welcome back, super sleuth."

Claire smiled. "I couldn't have done it without you, and your big strong muscles capturing Gordon like that."

"Is that all I am to you?" Ryan chuckled, a mischievous glint in his eyes. "A piece of meat?"

Claire laughed, shaking her head. She leaned in, pressing her lips against his in a tender kiss. The children mimicked vomiting sounds, causing Claire and Ryan to break apart, their laughter mingling with their playful disgust.

"You're so much more than that, Ryan Tyler," Claire said, her voice soft and sincere. "Thank you for never making me wonder where we stand with each other. All this business with Betty and Gordon… I feel lucky that we're us."

"I'm the lucky one," he said, a gentle smile tugging at his lips. "I know it's earlier than we planned, but should we head back tomorrow?"

Claire nodded, her heart swelling with the thought of home.

"I couldn't think of a better plan," she said. "But before we do, I have one more visit to make."

CHAPTER TWENTY-TWO

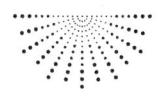

A smile played on Claire's lips as she watched Mrs Beaton twirl and sway in a sparkling red dress. The elderly woman's voice, still rich and powerful despite her age, filled the lounge of Oakwood with the soaring notes of an opera aria. Sunlight streamed through the windows, catching the sequins on her dress and casting glittering reflections across the walls and faces of the enraptured audience.

Some of the residents, inspired by the music, had risen from their seats and were now swaying in slow circles, their movements guided by the rhythm of Mrs Beaton's song. Claire felt a tear prick at the corner of her eye, moved by the joy and life that had been breathed into the room.

Celia crouched by Claire, a warm smile on her face.

"I wanted to thank you for leaving that scrapbook of Mrs Beaton's past with us," she said in a low voice. "It's helped us understand her a little better, and it gave me an idea of how we could bring her some joy."

"I'm glad it could help."

"I found that dress in a charity shop," Celia continued, gesturing towards the sparkling red gown. "It reminded me of one of the dresses in those old newspaper clippings. Mrs Beaton said the original was black. Still, she seems to love it."

Mrs Beaton spun around, the skirt of her dress flaring out and catching the light. The sequins sparkled like a glitter ball, scattering flecks of light across the room and drawing delighted gasps from the audience.

"Thank you for being patient with her. I know she can be a handful."

"Understatement, but it's what we're here to do. She's clearly very special to you. I'm glad she has some family."

"We were neighbours," Claire reminded her, "but I can't remember a time when she wasn't there."

"That sounds like family to me." She stood up, patting Claire's shoulder. "I'll keep a special eye on her for you."

With a final smile and a nod, Celia left Claire to watch as Mrs Beaton finished her song. Polite applause scattered the room, with Claire clapping the loudest in a standing ovation. Mrs Beaton stepped down from the makeshift stage, a wide smile on her face as she shuffled towards them.

"How was it?" Mrs Beaton asked, sounding unsure.

"Your best performance yet."

"Hmm. We'll see what the write-up says."

"I'm sure it'll be as glittering as your new frock."

"Between you and me," she said, pulling Claire in with a finger, "red has never been my colour, but my dreadful mother made me wear it."

"Right." Claire wondered if she should correct her, to let her know she'd long since escaped her mother's managerial clutches, but she didn't want to confuse her after her big comeback. "Well, I think you look beautiful. I only wish I could stay longer."

"You get yourself home, Claire." Mrs Beaton reached out and patted Claire's hand, her eyes twinkling with mischief. "And you take good care of my house now, you hear?"

A lump formed in Claire's throat, knowing Sally hadn't been able to work her mortgage miracles. But she didn't have the heart to tell her, not when she looked so happy and content.

"I will, Mrs Beaton. I promise."

"Now, go and tell the bartender I'll take a gin and tonic in my cabin," she whispered, "and if my mother comes looking for me, you haven't seen me."

"You know, I don't think she will."

"Has she finally thrown herself overboard?" Mrs Beaton let out a dry chuckle, shaking her head. "I might just do the same one of these days."

With a final wave over her shoulder, Mrs Beaton shuffled off towards her bedroom, and promising it wouldn't be too long until her next visit, Claire set off back towards the village.

THE CAFÉ WAS ALIGHT WITH GOSSIP AS VILLAGERS dissected the case. Claire navigated through the crowd, catching snippets of conversation as she made her way towards Julia.

"I heard it was the paramedic working on her own," one woman whispered to her friend.

"No, no, it was definitely the ex-husband," another countered, shaking his head. "Jealousy, I tell you."

Sue and Jessie rushed around, balancing trays laden with steaming cups of tea and plates of cakes. Despite the chaos, Julia caught Claire's eye, making her way over.

"I wanted to give you something before I left," Claire said, reaching into her bag and pulling out a small candle. "I cobbled this together using ingredients from Evelyn's pantry along with some scents I brought. I think—I *hope* —it captures the essence of this place. I was inspired the moment I stepped foot in here. Needs some time to cure before you can light it, but what do you think?"

Julia took the candle, breathing in the warm, inviting scent. Her eyes widened in delight.

"Coffee, brown sugar and... is that a hint of cinnamon?"

Claire nodded, grinning. "When I get back to Northash, I'm going to make a whole batch and feature it as my Star Candle of the Month. I'll send you a box."

"It's wonderful, Claire. Really wonderful. You're clearly skilled at your craft. I'd love that," Julia said, her smile widening. "And I have something for you, too." She ducked behind the counter and emerged with a small, neatly wrapped package. "I baked you a cake." She flipped back the lid and it was decorated with the words 'With love, from Mowgli.' "A thank you for finding him."

Claire accepted the package, touched by the gesture.

"He would have turned up. For all her faults, Mrs Beaton knows how to take care of a cat, especially the ones that aren't hers."

They stepped outside, the cool breeze a welcome respite from the bustling café. Julia pulled Claire into a warm hug.

"Don't be a stranger," Claire said as they parted. "The invitation is always open for you to visit Northash."

"I'll take you up on that," Julia promised, her eyes

twinkling. "Safe travels, Claire, and thanks for the candle. I'll keep an eye out for that box."

With a final wave, Claire turned and headed towards the B&B, the cake tucked safely under her arm and the scent of her new candle lingering in the air.

"Oh, my dears, I'm going to miss you all so much!" Evelyn announced as she draped crystal necklaces around Amelia and Hugo's necks, the stones glinting in the sunlight. "These will protect you on your journey home."

Greta and Eugene stood by the door, their bags packed and ready.

"I'm itching to get behind the wheel again," Eugene urged, bouncing on the balls of his feet. "I promise I'll drive much better than on the way down."

Greta raised an eyebrow, a smirk playing on her lips.

"I'll believe it when I see it, love."

Outside, Claire paused, taking in the place one last time. The sun cast a golden glow over the postcard-perfect quaint cottages and the busy café. Despite the darker underbelly she'd uncovered during her stay, Claire couldn't help but feel a sense of fondness for Peridale.

After they piled into the car, Eugene turned the key,

and the engine sputtered before stalling. Laughter filled the air as he tried again, this time with success.

"Back to Northash we go!" he declared.

"I believe in you, dear," Greta said. "Just... take it slow."

As they drove through the village, Dot and Percy waved from the green, their dogs yapping excitedly at their feet. They all waved back before turning up a winding country lane and away from the village. Claire took one last look at the green in the rear-view mirror, sure she'd be back one day.

CHAPTER TWENTY-THREE

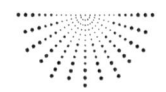

As the spring showers pelted down from the grey sky above, Eugene slowed the car to a crawl outside Claire's Candles. Claire braced herself for one final jolt of the handbrake, but to her surprise, Eugene brought the vehicle to a smooth stop. Exhaling with relief, Claire gazed at her candle shop, a sense of contentment washing over her despite the gloomy weather.

They sprung from the car and rushed inside, eager to escape the rain. As Claire stepped into her shop, she was delighted to see it bustling with customers, exactly as she had left it—albeit sparkling to within an inch of its life. Janet and Alan were manning the counter, while Damon added more lavender candles to the central display. He abandoned the restocking at the sight of her and greeted her with a tight hug.

"Aren't you a sight for sore eyes?" he said, squeezing hard. "That was the longest week of my life. Welcome back."

"And I brought cake," Claire announced, flipping open the box she carried. "And it's a good cake."

"'With love from Mow...'" Damon read the inscription. "Who's 'Mow'?"

"I already had a slice, and it's a long story. I'll tell you later." Taking a moment to survey her surroundings, Claire marvelled at the pristine state of her shop. "I can't believe everything is exactly how I left it."

Damon shifted his weight, a sheepish grin on his face.

"Oh, it wasn't... Your mum did rearrange everything. Several times, actually." He inhaled as though he was about to recount every trial he had suffered over the past week, but shook his head and let out the breath. "I let her do what she needed to do, but I stayed late last night with Sally and we put it all back as it was."

"You're a legend."

"Your mother wasn't too pleased this morning when she saw," he said, glancing towards Janet, busy behind the counter at the till while Alan bagged up. "I finally stood my ground."

"How did she take it?"

"Surprisingly fine."

"She's all bark and no bite." She winked. "Thank you, Damon. I don't know what I'd do without you."

After closing and a reunion with the cats in her—now show home clean—flat, Claire joined the others gathered around the shop counter to dig into the leftovers of Julia's cake.

"Delicious," Janet remarked. "It's even better than any of that vegan stuff they serve at Marley's café." She glanced at Eugene apologetically. "No offence, Eugene."

"None taken." Eugene chuckled. "I wish I could disagree with you, but this is scrumptious. It's a shame Julia's shop is so far away, eh? Though I think my waistline appreciates the distance. I don't know how everyone in Peridale isn't the size of a house with cakes like these on their doorstep."

"Speaking of Peridale," Alan said, "I see you haven't brought back a trophy."

"Oh, yes," Janet said, arching a brow. "You've spoken about nothing else for months on end, Greta."

Greta shrugged. "We came third. Given what we were up against, I can't complain."

"All those murders did throw us off our game," Eugene said, twisting his wrist around, "and my injury didn't help."

"I was more talking about Claire's technique." Greta

chuckled at Claire, a mischievous glint in her eye. "In the end, you turned out to be a rather decent player. Have you thought about joining our team full-time? We meet every Thursday."

Claire pondered the question for a moment, but she shook her head—as much fun as she had ended up having, her passions lay elsewhere.

"Maybe in three or so decades," she replied, forking the last of her slice into her mouth. "For now, I'm happy to get back to what I do best. And speaking of which, if everyone doesn't mind, I'd like some time alone to get started on my next star candle batch." She closed the lid of the cake box. "Damon, get thinking about a coffee-inspired window display, will you? I want this place to look and smell like a café ripped out of the Cotswolds."

As the others began to disperse, Claire cleared away the forks, with only Ryan and the children remaining. While Amelia and Hugo gathered the ingredients from the meticulously organised shelves, Claire's phone buzzed with a text message.

> SALLY
> Meet me at the cul-de-sac in an hour.

"Anything important?" Ryan asked, handing her a tiny cup brimming with a double espresso shot.

"I'm not sure."

They arrived at the cul-de-sac, sending Amelia and Hugo off to let themselves into Claire's parents' house. Outside Mrs Beaton's house, Sally waited beneath a giant umbrella, the rain pattering against the fabric.

"Come on in," Sally called out, ushering them towards the front door.

As they hurried inside, Claire couldn't help but wonder what this unexpected meeting was all about.

"Sally, if you're just taunting us..."

"Would I ever?" Sally said cryptically. "If you'll come through."

They made their way to the dated kitchen, where a crisp white envelope waited on the peeling vinyl countertop. Sally picked it up and handed it to Claire, her eyes sparkling with barely contained excitement.

"Open it."

With trembling fingers, Claire tore open the envelope, revealing a mortgage offer from a broker.

"What's this?"

"It's yours," Sally said, biting her lip. "The house. It's yours if you want it."

"But how?" Ryan folded his arms, reading the offer over Claire's shoulder. "You said you couldn't make it work."

"And *I* couldn't. But I pinky promised you a miracle, and someone out there must have been listening." Sally's grin widened as she paused, savouring the moment. "The people handling the sale on Mrs Beaton's behalf received a very stern phone call from the lady herself with two new conditions."

Claire and Ryan exchanged a bewildered look.

"Spit it out," Claire ordered, the paper rustling in her trembling hands.

"First," Sally continued, "the house value was to be lowered by £50,000, bringing it way, way under market value, and it was already a bargain. The handlers tried to fight it, but Mrs Beaton was adamant. And second, only people named 'Claire' could put in an offer at that price."

A burst of laughter escaped Claire's lips, the absurdity and wonder of the situation sinking in.

"Batty Old Beaton," she murmured, shaking her head in disbelief. "Before I left, the last thing she said to me was to look after this place. I… I can't believe it."

Sally reached into her bag and pulled out a bottle of champagne.

"Don't let this go to waste. It's the good stuff."

She produced a pen and held it out.

"It does need a lot of work," Ryan said as he surveyed the dated kitchen. "We'll have to do it slowly… live in it while we're renovating…"

"It won't be cheap." Claire nodded, her own doubts creeping in. "We don't really know what we're doing either."

"You'll learn," Sally urged, pushing the pen at them. "And no, it won't be easy… but in my professional opinion—and I'm not making a penny on commission from this—don't let this pass you by. It's a golden opportunity… one I know you both want."

Without taking another second to think about it, Claire accepted the pen, her hand steadying as she signed the paperwork against the counter. Ryan followed suit, his signature joining hers on the life-changing document.

With a triumphant grin, Sally popped the cork on the champagne bottle, the bubbles frothing over the neck.

"To Mrs Beaton," she said, raising the bottle in a toast before taking a swig and passing it over, "and to a new chapter."

Claire sipped the fizz, nestling in Ryan's embrace as her heart fluttered in her chest.

"To a new chapter," Ryan echoed, raising the bottle.

"A new chapter," Claire said, taking in the kitchen that mirrored the shape of the homes she and Ryan had both grown up in a stone's throw away. "Right where it all began."

Thank you for reading, and don't forget to
RATE/REVIEW!

The Claire's Candles story continues in the 11th book..

SPICED ORANGE SUSPICION
COMING OCTOBER 29th 2024

WANT TO BE KEPT UP TO DATE WITH AGATHA FROST RELEASES? *SIGN UP THE FREE NEWSLETTER!*

www.AgathaFrost.com

You can also follow **Agatha Frost** across social media. Search 'Agatha Frost' on:

Facebook
Twitter
Goodreads
Instagram

ALSO BY AGATHA FROST

Claire's Candles

11. Spiced Orange Suspicion

10. Double Espresso Deception

9. Frosted Plum Fears

8. Wildflower Worries

7. Candy Cane Conspiracies

6. Toffee Apple Torment

5. Fresh Linen Fraud

4. Rose Petal Revenge

3. Coconut Milk Casualty

2. Black Cherry Betrayal

1. Vanilla Bean Vengeance

Peridale Cafe

32. Lemon Drizzle Loathing

31. Sangria and Secrets

30. Mince Pies and Madness

29. Pumpkins and Peril

28. Eton Mess and Enemies

27. Banana Bread and Betrayal

26. **Carrot Cake and Concern**

25. **Marshmallows and Memories**

24. **Popcorn and Panic**

23. **Raspberry Lemonade and Ruin**

22. **Scones and Scandal**

21. **Profiteroles and Poison**

20. **Cocktails and Cowardice**

19. **Brownies and Bloodshed**

18. **Cheesecake and Confusion**

17. **Vegetables and Vengeance**

16. **Red Velvet and Revenge**

15. **Wedding Cake and Woes**

14. **Champagne and Catastrophes**

13. **Ice Cream and Incidents**

12. **Blueberry Muffins and Misfortune**

11. **Cupcakes and Casualties**

10. **Gingerbread and Ghosts**

9. **Birthday Cake and Bodies**

8. **Fruit Cake and Fear**

7. **Macarons and Mayhem**

6. **Espresso and Evil**

5. **Shortbread and Sorrow**

4. **Chocolate Cake and Chaos**

3. Doughnuts and Deception

2. Lemonade and Lies

1. Pancakes and Corpses

Other

The Agatha Frost Winter Anthology

Peridale Cafe Book 1-10

Peridale Cafe Book 11-20

Claire's Candles Book 1-3

Printed in Great Britain
by Amazon